"No compromises this time. I'm sorry."

"Do what you want." She sighed, turning toward the door. "I find I don't really care!"

"For someone who professes not to care at all, Marnie, your actions—and reactions—say otherwise. Perhaps you care *too* much?"

"I will always despise you for forcing me into accepting you back like this! Is that what you want?" she asked. "A woman—a wife who will resent every moment she has to spend in your arms? Is the price you're going to pay for having me back in your life really worth the satisfaction you think you'll feel at managing it?"

"I know it will be."

MICHELLE REID grew up on the southern edges of Manchester, the youngest in a family of five lively children. She now lives in the beautiful county of Cheshire with her busy executive husband and two grown-up daughters. She loves reading, the ballet and playing tennis when she gets the chance. She hates cooking, cleaning and despises ironing! Sleep she can do without—she claims she produces some of her best writing during the early hours of the morning.

Books by Michelle Reid

HARLEQUIN PRESENTS PLUS

1615—HOUSE OF GLASS

HARLEQUIN PRESENTS

1440—A QUESTION OF PRIDE
1478—NO WAY TO BEGIN
1533—THE DARK SIDE OF DESIRE
1597—COERCION TO LOVE

HARLEQUIN ROMANCE

2994—EYE OF HEAVEN

MICHELLE REID

Lost in Love

Harlequin Books

TORONTO • NEW YORK • LONDON
AMSTERDAM • PARIS • SYDNEY • HAMBURG
STOCKHOLM • ATHENS • TOKYO • MILAN
MADRID • WARSAW • BUDAPEST • AUCKLAND

ISBN 0-373-11665-9

LOST IN LOVE

This edition published by arrangement with Harlequin Enterprises B. V.

Printed in U.S.A.

CHAPTER ONE

'No.' Marnie threw down her paintbrush and turned to find a rag to wipe the paint from her fingers. 'I won't do it,' she refused. 'And I don't know how you have the gall to ask me!'

Her brother's face was surly to say the least. 'I've got to have it by tomorrow or I've had it!' he cried. 'There isn't anyone else I know I can turn to. And if you asked him, he'd...'

'I said no.'

They glared at each other across the width of her studio, Marnie with her arms folded across her chest in that stubborn, immovable way her brother knew only too well, her cool gaze refusing to so much as glance at the arm he had wrapped in a white linen sling or the vivid bruise he was wearing down one side of his face.

She made an impatient flick with her hand. 'The last time you talked me into going begging to Guy, I had to stand there and endure a thirty-minute lecture on your weak character—and my own stupidity for pandering to it!' she reminded Jamie. 'I will not give him another chance to repeat that little scene—even if it does mean you having to face the music for a change!'

'I can't believe you're going to let me down like this!' Jamie cried. 'We both know Guy is still crazy about you! He can't refuse you a damned——'

'*Jamie*——!' she warned. Her relationship, hostile or otherwise, with Guy Frabosa was always a risky subject to get on to at the best of times, and her warning had her brother shifting uncomfortably where he stood.

'Well, it's true,' he mumbled, unable to hold her gaze. 'The last time it happened,' he persisted none the less, 'I admit it was my own stupid fault, and Guy was probably right to send me packing—but . . .'

'It wasn't *you* he sent packing,' his sister angrily pointed out. 'It was me! It wasn't *you* who had to listen to him verbally annihilate your family, it was me! And it certainly was not you who had to stand there taking it all firmly in the face without a word to say in your defence,' she concluded tightly. 'It was most definitely me!'

'Then let me try asking him——'

'You?' she scoffed, sending him a look fit to wither. Jamie was not one of Guy's most favourite people. In fact, it could be said that Jamie was Guy's least favourite person in the whole wide world! 'You must be feeling desperate if you're thinking of tackling the great man yourself,' she derided. 'He's liable to make mincement out of you in thirty seconds flat—*and* you know it.'

'But if you——'

'*No*——!'

'God, Marnie.' Jamie sank heavily into a chair, defeat sending his thin frame hunching over in distress.

Marnie hardened her heart against the pathetic picture he presented, determined not to weaken this time. It was no use, she told herself firmly. Guy was right. It was time Jamie learned to sort out his own messes. In the four years since she and Guy had parted, Jamie had sent her to him on no less than three occasions to beg on his behalf. That last time had brought Guy's well deserved wrath down on her head, and he had warned her then that the next time she came to him with her brother's problems he would expect something back in return. She had understood instantly what he meant. And there was just no way—*no way* she was going to put herself in that position. Not even for her brother.

'I'll lose everything,' Jamie murmured thickly.

'Good,' she said, not believing him for a moment. 'Perhaps once you have lost it you'll learn the importance of protecting what you had!'

'How can you be so mean?' he choked, lifting his wounded face from his uninjured hand to stare wretchedly at her. He just could not believe she was letting him down this time. 'You've become hard, Marnie,' he accused her, sending her the first look of dislike she had ever received from this only blood relative she had in the world. 'This business with Guy has made you hard.'

'Look...' She sighed, softening slightly because Jamie was right, she had become hard—a necessary shell grown around herself for self-protection. But she didn't want to hurt Jamie. She hated seeing anyone hurt. 'I can probably lay my hands on—ten thousand pounds by tomorrow if that's any good to you.'

'A drop in the ocean,' he mumbled ungratefully, and his sister flared all over again.

'Then what do you expect me to do?' she yelled. 'Sell my damned soul for you?' And that was what it would amount to if she went to Guy for money again. He would demand her soul as payment.

Her brother shook his head. 'God, you make me feel like a heel.'

'Well, that's something, I suppose.' She sighed. 'Why can't you think before you jump, Jamie?' On a gesture of exasperation, she dropped down on the sofa beside him. 'I mean,' she went on, her violet gaze impatient as she studied him, 'to drive a valuable car like that out on the road without insurance!'

The disgust in her voice made him flinch. 'I was delivering it,' he muttered defensively. 'I didn't expect a dirty great lorry to drive smack into the side of me!'

'But isn't that what insurance is for?' his sister mocked scathingly. 'To protect you against the unexpected?'

Her brother was a master at rebuilding very rare and very expensive old-model high-performance cars. It was probably his only saving grace—that and managing to catch and marry about the most sweetest creature on this earth. But this affinity he had with anything mechanical was something special. Marnie had seen him painstakingly take apart and put back together again everything from an old baby carriage to a vintage Rolls in his time.

'Guy has a 1955 Jaguar XK140 Drophead similar to the one I smashed up.' Never one to give up easily, Jamie was reminding her of a fact she had already remembered. 'He might, if you asked him, consider selling it to me on a long-term loan.'

Guy had a whole fleet of fast cars. It was one of his *grandes passions*, possessing cars with an awesome power under their bonnets. As an ex-Formula One racing car driver and world champion himself, his love of speed had once excited Marnie beyond bearing. There had been something incredibly stimulating in dicing with death at one-hundred-plus miles per hour. Guy had taken her out several times to share that kind of exciting feeling with him, his dark face vibrant with life, eyes flashing, mouth stretched into a devilish smile as he glanced—too often for her peace of mind—at her wide-eyed and anxious expression as their speed increased on surge after surge of fierce growling power. The next best thing to sex, he called it. And it certainly left them both on a high which could only be assuaged in one all-consuming way.

'Please, Marnie . . .' Her brother's voice shook with desperation. 'You've got to help me out on this one!'

'I can't believe you drove a car of that value out on the roads without bothering to insure it!' she snapped out angrily.

Jamie lifted his hands in an empty gesture. 'It wasn't that I didn't bother, I just—forgot,' he admitted. 'You know what I'm like, sis, when I get engrossed in something.' His blue eyes pleaded for understanding. 'I tend to forget everything else!'

'Including your responsibility to the poor fool who trusted you with his precious car!'

Jamie winced and she let out an impatient sigh. 'The last time you got yourself in a mess, it was because you went over budget and omitted to warn your client that it was going to cost him several thousand more than you quoted!'

'I don't do half a job!' he haughtily defended that particular criticism. 'He wanted his car looking like new, so I rebuilt it to look like new.'

'Then he refused to take delivery of it until you cut down the bill—which you refused to do. Which meant Guy had to step in and sort the mess out—yet again!'

'You know as well as I do that Guy made on the deal in the end,' Jamie derided that accusation. 'The crafty devil bought the damned car from the man at less than it was worth, and put it into his own collection! It cost me fifteen thousand pounds to put that car back together, of which I saw only ten!'

'And two thousand of that I lent to you and never saw again!'

'OK—OK...' Jamie sighed, making a weary retreat by getting up from the sofa to lope over to the window where a bright June sun was beginning to ruin what light she had left of the morning to paint by. 'So, I'm a lousy businessman. You don't have to rub it in.'

Marnie looked at him in impatient sympathy. He was quite right. He was a lousy businessman. He was like the proverbial absent-minded professor when he got his head beneath the bonnet of a new challenge. But she'd thought he'd got himself together in the business department over the last year since Clare had taken over that side of things for him.

She frowned at that last thought, wondering why Clare hadn't made sure his insurance was up to date. It wasn't like her sister-in-law to forget something as basic as that.

'If you won't help me, Marnie,' Jamie murmured into the dull silence that was throbbing all around them, 'I don't know what I'm going to do. The guy is threatening nasty reprisals if I don't come up with his money.'

'Oh, Jamie!' she sighed, leaning forward to rub her forehead with a hand.

'But that's not all...'

No? she wondered cynically. Could there *be* more?

'It's Clare,' he said.

'Clare?' Her head shot away from her hand.

'She's—she's pregnant again.'

'What—already?' Instant concern darkened his sister's eyes, her face going pale as she stared at him. 'Isn't it a bit too soon?' she whispered.

'Yes,' he sighed, turning to look at her, then, sighing again, he came back to throw himself down next to her. 'Too damn soon for anyone's peace of mind...'

Marnie swallowed, her anger with her brother evaporating with this new and far more worrying concern. Clare had gone through what could only be described as a woman's worst nightmare, having lost her first baby right on the three-month borderline the experts liked to call safe. Safe. She scorned it bitterly. There was no such thing as safe during a nine-month-long confinement. Fate and Mother Nature saw to that.

The doctors had warned them not to rush straight into trying for another. 'Give your body time to heal,' they'd advised. 'And your hearts time to grieve.'

'How—how far is she?' She could hardly speak for the hard lump which had formed in her throat.

'Two months.' Jamie glanced at her, his thin face strained. 'Marnie... You have to understand now that this has all come at a bad time for me. I can't afford to let Clare know about this.' He dropped his head, giving his sandy hair a frustrated tug. 'She's worried half out of her mind as it is, wondering, frightened...'

She swallowed, nodding, unable to say a single word.

'If you could just find it in yourself to help me out of this one—I swear to you, Marnie,' he promised huskily, 'I swear on the——'

'Don't say it!' she rasped, her hand shaking as it snapped out to grip tightly at his wrist. 'Don't even think it!'

'God, no!' he groaned, shuddering when he realised just what he had been going to say. 'Hell—I don't know what's happening to me,' he choked. 'I can't think straight for worrying about Clare, never mind this mess with the Jag. I——'

'Is this why you weren't insured?' she asked with sudden insight. 'Has Clare stopped doing all the clerical work since she suspected she was pregnant?'

Jamie nodded. 'God,' he went on distractedly, 'it was bad enough me having to walk into the flat with this arm in a sling, and my face in this kind of mess—she almost fainted in fright!' A ragged sigh shot from him. 'I didn't dare tell her she'd forgotten to renew my insurance! She'd have . . .' His voice trailed off, and they both sat, their hearts thumping heavily in their breasts.

'All right,' Marnie murmured huskily. 'I'll go and see Guy today.'

Jamie's relief was so palpable that it was almost worth it—almost. Jamie had no idea—couldn't know what this was going to cost her.

'Listen, tell Guy I've found a brilliant MG K3 Magnette!' he said urgently, trying his best to make up for putting her in this position. 'Tell—tell him he can have it for his collection when it's finished,' he offered. 'It isn't as good as the one he's already got, and it won't cover the debt I'll owe him, but...' he swallowed, emotion thickening his voice '...I'll pay him back every penny this time, Marnie. That's a promise. And thank you—thank you for doing this for me this one last time.'

'I'm doing it for Clare, not for you.' Why she'd said that Marnie wasn't about to analyse, but the way her brother's face paled she knew the remark had cut—as, perhaps, it had meant to. But at this moment Marnie found she hated every single one of the male race.

'I know that,' he said, getting up. 'I know both you and Guy don't think my neck worth saving.'

'That's not true, and you know it,' Marnie sighed, softening her manner slightly. 'But I do think it's about time you took care of your own affairs properly, Jamie—and by that I mean yourself, and not leaving it all to Clare.'

'I mean to from now on.' He sounded so determined that Marnie was surprised into believing him. 'After all, she's going to have enough on her plate with—everything else.'

He was by the door, eager to leave now he'd got that promise from Marnie. 'Will—will you give me a call as soon as you've spoken to Guy?' It was tentatively said, but insistent all the same, and Marine glanced sharply at him.

'That urgent, huh?' she drawled.

He nodded and flushed. 'The man is riding on my back,' he admitted.

Just as you are riding on mine, Marnie thought as she watched him go. Then took back that thought with a bitter twist to her tensely held mouth. It was unworthy. She loved her brother, and for once the mess he was in was not of his own making but poor Clare's.

Clare...her eyes clouded over as she thought of her pretty little sister-in-law and the minefield of anxieties she must be negotiating right now. And Jamie was right; Clare was not in any fit condition to take any more stress.

Even if it meant Marnie placing herself in the hands of the enemy!

A shiver rippled through her, leaving her cold even though the sun was warm in the room, the unwanted memories managing to crawl through the thick protective casing she wore around herself, sending her blue eyes bleak as the artist in her began to construct his image in front of her.

Guy, she thought achingly, unable to stop the picture from building. A big man, but lean and muscular, with the kind of naturally tanned skin that enhanced his dark good looks. His chocolate-brown eyes always made exciting promises, and that lazy, sexy smile he used to save for her alone could... She gave an inner sigh that stayed just this side of pain. Her dark Italian love, she remembered wistfully. The only man who had ever managed to get her soul to leave her body and soar on an eddying wave of pure exquisite feeling.

Guy was a man of the earth and air, with banked-down fires inside him that would flare and turn the blood to sizzling, spitting flames.

He was the kind of man whose charismatic power over the opposite sex had given him an arrogance few would deny him. His huge ego was well deserved—

along with his colourful reputation. Guy was a man's idea of a man—the kind of man who walked right out of a woman's foolish dreams. And a selfish, cruel and faithless swine! she reminded herself bitterly. He saw what he wanted, and took it with all the fire and passion in his hot Latin nature—just as he had seen and taken her! In his arrogance, he'd made her fall in love with him, then ruthlessly and callously thrown that love right back in her face! She would never forgive him for that. Never.

Four years ago, Guy had hurt her so deeply that she had prayed never to set eyes on him again. But with his usual arrogance he had refused to allow her that one small relief. And, four years on, they now shared a different kind of relationship, one which had them tiptoeing around each other like wary adversaries, using their tongues instead of their bodies to strike sparks off each other. Hostile yet close—oddly close. In the four long years since she and Guy had split up in a blaze of pain and anger, he had not allowed her to cut him out of her life. Guy possessed a tenacity which surprised her somewhat. For a man who was able to get whatever he wished at the simple click of his fingers, it seemed odd to her that he should still want her. She was, after all, one of his few failures in life, and his ego did not usually like being reminded of those.

Now, and for the first time in a long time, she sensed her own vulnerability, and another smile touched her mouth—one full of rueful whimsy this time. Guy had always predicted that Jamie would be the source of her inevitable downfall.

It seemed that his years of patience were about to bear fruit.

She glanced across the mad clutter of her busy studio room to where the telephone sat innocent and inert on the small table by the door, and slowly, carefully she steadied her emotions, settled her features into their normal cool, calm mask, and readied herself for what was to come. For Jamie might be placing her on a plate for Guy, but it did not mean she was going to sit still on it!

With these defiant thoughts to accompany her across the room, Marnie lifted the receiver off its rest and began to dial the never-to-be-forgotten number of *il signor* Guy Frabosa's London home.

CHAPTER TWO

HE WASN'T there.

'Typical,' Marnie muttered as she replaced the receiver, 'just damned typical!' feeling all that careful mental preparation going frustratingly to waste.

Guy might live in London, have his business base there, but the very nature of that business kept him constantly on the move, personally overseeing every aspect of the conglomerate of companies he had inherited from his abdicating father on Guy's own retirement from motor racing. And it took several calls to different numbers suggested to her before she eventually tracked him down, in Edinburgh of all places.

She was put through to a plastic-sounding female voice who seemed about as approachable as a polar bear. 'Mr Frabosa is in conference,' came the uncompromising block to Marie's request to speak to him. 'He does not wish to be disturbed.'

Is that so? mused Marnie, the woman's frigid tone putting a mulish glint into her blue eyes. For the last hour she had been passed from pillar to post in her attempt to contact Guy, and in the end she had only got the Edinburgh information by pulling rank on the frosty-voiced female blocking her request. It wasn't often that Marnie laid claim to her married title, but she felt no qualms about doing so when she thought the moment warranted it. She had more than earned the right, after all.

And it seemed the same tactic was required again! 'Just inform him that *Mrs* Frabosa wishes to speak to him, will you?' she said coldly, and gained the expected result as the woman stammered through a nervous apology and went off to inform Guy of his caller.

For the next five minutes, she hung on the line with only the intermittent crackle of static to tell her she was still connected while she waited for Guy to come dutifully to the phone.

He didn't.

Instead she got the plastic voice again, sounding flustered. 'Mr Frabosa sends his apologies, Mrs Frabosa, but asks if he could call you back as soon as he returns to London?'

Marnie's lips tightened. 'When will that be exactly?' she asked.

'The day after tomorrow, Mrs Frabosa.'

The day after tomorrow. Marnie paused for a moment to consider her next move. The very fact that she was calling him must in itself tell Guy that she needed to speak to him urgently, since it was such a rare occurrence. It was typical, she irritably supposed, for him to make her wait. He always had liked to annoy her by stretching her patience to its limits.

Well, two could play at this game, she decided, as sly calculation joined the sense of mutiny. 'Then tell him thank you, but it doesn't matter,' she announced, and calmly replaced the receiver.

She knew Guy, she knew him well.

It took just three minutes for him to get back to her. And, just to annoy him, she waited until she had counted six hollow rings before she lifted the receiver and casually chanted her name.

'Sometimes, *cara*, you try my patience just a little too far.'

The deep velvet tones of his voice swimming so smoothly down the line had her closing her eyes and clenching her teeth in an effort to stop herself responding to the sheer beauty of it. Loving or hating this man, he still had the power to move her sexually.

'Hello, Guy. How are you?' Of the people who knew him in England—his adopted country since his father emigrated here some decades ago—most called him Guy with a hard G. Marnie, on the other hand, had always preferred the European pronunciation, and the way the softer-sounding 'ghee' slid so sensually off the tongue. And Guy loved it. He said just hearing her say his name was enough to make his body respond to the promise it seemed to offer. Once upon a time she would say his name just to witness that unhidden burning response. Now she said it to annoy him because he was well aware it held no invitation any more.

'I am well, Marnie,' he politely replied, before going on to wryly mock, 'Right up until I heard you wished to speak to me, that is.'

'Poor darling,' she mourned, quite falsely. 'What a troublesome ex-wife you have.'

'Is that what you're going to be?' he enquired. 'Troublesome?'

'Probably,' she admitted, keeping her voice light. It always paid to be in control around Guy; he was just too quick to turn the slightest sign of weakness to his own advantage. And the advantage was going to be with him all too soon enough. 'It's rather important that I see you today. Can it be arranged?'

'Not unless you can get to Edinburgh,' he told her bluntly. 'I will be stuck here for at least another two days.'

Marnie suppressed an impatient sigh. Could Jamie's problem wait that long? Going by the sense of urgency her brother had brought in with him that afternoon, the answer was no, it would not wait.

Marnie chewed on her bottom lip, considering calling his bluff a second time and just severing the conversation with a light, 'Shame, but no matter, forget I even called,' kind of reply. It had worked several times in the past. They might be divorced, but not with Guy's blessing. He had fought her all the way, until she had turned totally ruthless and used her trump card against him. But he made no secret of the fact that he was quite willing to do almost anything for her but die at her feet, and usually when she snapped her fingers he came running.

Then she remembered Clare, and any idea of playing cat and mouse with Guy on this one slid quietly and irrevocably from her mind.

'I suppose you have your plane up there with you?' she said.

'Correct, my love,' he said quite happily. Guy liked to thwart her when possible. She allowed it to happen so rarely that he tended to wallow in the few occasions when it did occur. 'Of course,' he went on, his velvet voice smoothly mocking, 'if the idea of flying shuttle up here is totally abhorrent to you, then I think I can put Sunday afternoon aside for you...'

And what about Saturday? she wondered, feeling the biting discomfort of evil suspicion creep insidiously through her blood. Today was Wednesday. He said he was stuck up there for two days. That brought him to Friday. That could only mean one thing in Guy's book, for he had this—unbroken little rule about never spending Saturday alone! He most probably had her with him now! Her suspicious mind took her on another step. After all, hadn't she personal experience of Guy's passions? One night without a woman and he wasn't fit to know!

'And I also suppose you are entertaining one of your *ladies* up there?'

'Am I?' he murmured in a maddeningly unrevealing drawl.

'If I make the effort to get to Edinburgh, Guy,' she went on tightly, 'it will not be to play gooseberry to your latest fancy piece!'

'Darling,' he drawled, silky-voiced, refusing to be riled by her frankly aggravating tone, 'if you can take so much trouble just to share my company, then I will make sure I am free.'

Which still told her exactly nothing! 'And the poor fool who is living under the mistaken belief that she will be enjoying your full attention—what happens to her?'

'Why?' he countered. 'Are you expecting to stay with me all night?' He sounded insufferably at ease, mildly surprised, and horribly mocking. 'If that is the case, darling, then I most certainly will make sure I am free.'

Marnie's lips tightened. 'If you're still hankering after that, Guy,' she told him witheringly, 'then I feel sorry for you. I happen to be rather fastidious about the men who share my bed. One cannot be too careful these days.'

'Bitch,' he said. 'Take care, Marnie, that one day I don't decide to prove to you just how weak your aversion to me actually is, because you would never forgive yourself for surrendering to this—now, what was it you once called me?' He was playing the silky snake now, slithering along her nerve-ends with that lethal weapon of a tongue of his. 'A middle-aged has-been putting himself out for voluntary stud? Quaint,' he drawled. 'Very quaint.'

Marnie had the grace to wince at the hard reminder of those particular words. She had flung some terrible things at him four years ago. Unforgivable things, most of them. But she had been hurting so badly at the time, while he had been so calm, so utterly gentle with her that she had simply exploded, wanting to rile his sleeping devil with terrible insults and bitter accusations. She had not succeeded. All she had achieved was to make him walk abruptly away from her. It was either that or hit her, she knew that now. But four years ago his turning his back on her at that moment had hurt almost as much as everything else he had done to her.

'It isn't my fault you crave variety,' she put in waspishly to hide her own discomfort.

'It is that same "craving", as you so sweetly put it,' he countered, 'that made our nights such—exquisite adventures.'

'And I was so endearingly naïve, wasn't I?' Her full bottom lip curled in derision. 'Such a pathetically gullible thing, and so willing to let you walk all over me.'

'Look.' His patience suddenly snapped. 'I really have no more time to give to this kind of verbal battle today. If you called me up just to fill in a few spare moments trying to irritate me, then I think I should inform you that you have managed it. Now,' he said curtly, 'do you come up to Edinburgh or do we sever this conversation before it deteriorates into a real slanging match?'

'I'll check the times of the shuttle and let your secretary know my arrival time,' she muttered, backing down. It would do her cause no good to have put him in one of his black moods before she'd even got to see him. Things were going to be difficult enough as it was.

'I think I should also mention at this juncture that if this has anything to do with that brother of yours then you will be wasting your time taking that shuttle,' he warned.

'I'll see you later,' she said, and heard his sigh of impatience as she quickly replaced the receiver.

Jamie must have been standing by the telephone waiting for her to call, because he answered it on the first ring. 'Clare's resting upstairs,' he explained. 'I didn't want the telephone to disturb her. Have you spoken to Guy?'

'He's in Edinburgh,' she informed him. 'I'm on my way up to see him right now.'

'Thanks for doing this for me, Marnie,' he murmured gruffly. 'I know how much you hate going to him for anything, and believe me, I wouldn't have asked you to do it this time if it weren't for Clare . . .'

'How is she?' Marnie enquired concernedly.

'Tense,' her brother clipped. 'Over-bright. Pretending she's worrying about nothing, when really she's so afraid of doing the wrong thing that she barely makes a move without giving it careful consideration first.'

'Yes,' murmured Marnie, well aware of all Clare's painful heart-searching after that first miscarriage. She could understand how a woman must inevitably put the blame upon herself. Common sense and all the doctors in the world might tell you that it was just one of those natural tragedies that happened in life, but no matter how hard you tried you could never quite convince yourself of that. The feelings of guilt still tormented you day and night.

'If we can just get her through this next vital month, then maybe she'll begin to believe it's going to be all right this time . . .'

'Well, give her my love,' Marnie said. 'And just make sure you don't give her anything else to worry about.'

'I'm not a complete fool, Marnie,' her brother said tightly. 'I do know when I'm standing right on the bottom line.'

Well, that was something, Marnie supposed on an inner sigh. Perhaps—perhaps, she considered hopefully, this double crisis could just be the making of her scatter-brained, preoccupied brother. 'I'll give you a call the moment Guy decides what he's going to do about it all,' she assured him. 'You just take good care of Clare.'

'I intend to,' he said firmly. 'And—thanks again for doing this for me.'

'Don't thank me, Jamie,' Marnie sighed a little wearily. 'Thank Guy—if he agrees to help you out of this one.'

No one knowing only the Marnie Western-Frabosa who was the beautiful but very Bohemian-styled artist usually dressed in a paint smudged T-shirt and faded jeans would recognise her in the elegant creature who came gracefully through the Arrivals gate at Edinburgh Airport late that same afternoon.

To the man whose lazy black eyes followed her progress across the busy concourse she represented everything he desired in a woman. The first time he had ever set eyes on her had been enough to make his jaded senses throb with a need to possess, solely and totally. Five long and eventful years had passed by since then, and he still could not control that dragging clutch at his loins simply gazing at her caused.

Her skin was pure peaches and cream, so perfect, it fascinated. Her hair, long and finely spun, had been twisted in a knot on top of her head today, but the severity of the style could not dim the thousand and one different shades of reds and golds running through it. It shimmered in the overhead lights. Hers was a rich and golden beauty, made more enchanting by the pure oval of her softly featured face. Her eyes were blue—the shade of blue that could blaze purple with passion or icy grey with anger. Her nose was small and straight—with just the slightest tendency to look haughty when she lifted her chin a certain defiant way. And her mouth...he studied her mouth, lifted slightly at the corners at the moment by some rueful thought she was considering—that mouth had to be the most sensually evocative mouth he had ever seen. The fact that he knew it felt and tasted even more exciting than it looked did not ease the slow burn at present taking place low in his gut.

She was wearing purple, a colour that had always suited her. It was nothing but a simple off-the-peg cotton jersey dress, but it did wonderful things for her figure, hugging the curving shape of her body from neck to hip to just above the curve of her slender knees, leaving little work left to the imagination. And long, slender legs he knew from experience did not stop until they reached her waist brought her onwards towards him with an inbuilt sensual grace which put a smouldering glint in his hooded eyes.

Marnie saw the gleam as she made eye-to-eye contact with the darkly handsome and dangerously charismatic Guy Frabosa.

Sired by an Italian father to a French mother, brought up from the age of ten in England, then having spent most of his adult life frequenting most of the major countries in the world, Guy should have considered himself very cosmopolitan, yet he considered himself Italian to the very last drop of blood in his veins. And perhaps he was right to do so, since it was the Italian side of his breeding that burned through him like a warning beacon to any woman receptive to sheer male virility.

Of course, he, in his conceit, did pander to it, using the liquid smoothness of his Italian accent as one of his most effective weapons, refusing stubbornly to allow it to give way to his superb grasp of the English language, so the 'r's rolled off his tongue like purrs, sexy enough to make any woman quiver.

He was tall, powerfully built yet surprisingly lithe with it. A figure to hang fine clothes on, good quality hand-made clothes with a cut to suit the man—exclusive. His Latin black hair had given way to silver at the temples but that only added to his attraction rather than diminished it. For a thirty-nine-year-old man who had lived every single one of those years to its fullest potential, Guy still packed a fair punch in the solar plexus. He was one of those lucky men who improved with the years—like fine wine, he matured instead of ageing. Eyes of a dark, dark brown were generally lazily sensual, but could, if he wanted them to, harden to cold black pebbles which could freeze out the most tenacious foe. His nose was long and thin—not slim, thin, with a tendency to flare at the nostrils. Arrogant, and, like the rock-hard set of his chin, a direct warning to the ruthless streak in his character. Whereas his mouth by contrast was truly sensual, a very expressive tool he used to convey his moods, thin and tight when angry, sardonically twisted when mildly amused, a wide and attractive frame to perfect white teeth when touched into full-blown laughter, and soft, full and passionate when sexually aroused.

Then there was that other mouth, the one he saved for Marnie alone. The one he was wearing right at this moment as he watched her approach him through the mill of commuter bodies.

It was the half-soft, half-twisted, half-smiling mouth that said he didn't really know how to feel about her, and really never had.

That, Marnie thought as she carefully doused down her own inevitable response to this first glimpse of him—that deep and all-consuming inner recognition of her body's perfect master—was and always had been her most powerful weapon over Guy: his inability to decide just where she fitted into his life. He had once thought he'd done it, fitted her neatly into the box marked 'wife', of the forbearing and dutiful kind. Blindly besotted, safely caught and netted—only to find out, when he tried testing the springs of his trap, that he had made the biggest mistake of his life.

She reached him, waited calmly for his dark eyes to make their slow and lazy climb of her body from soft purple suede shoes to the scoop-necked top of her simple dress. Then they lifted to wryly take in the proud tilt to her chin, her mouth, heart-shaped and slightly mocking, along the straight line of her small nose until at last clashing with the full and striking blueness of her eyes.

The muscles around her stomach quivered. Standing this close to him, it was impossible not to respond to the raw beauty of Guy's face.

'Marnie,' he murmured.

'Hello, Guy,' she quietly replied, smiling a little, because even though she hated him she loved him, if it was possible to feel the two emotions at the same time.

He knew it too, which put that look of rueful irony in his eyes as he took another step to close the gap between them. Guy was Italian enough to express a greeting with a kiss on both cheeks, and Marnie had long since given up trying to deter him. So she stood calmly waiting for the embrace with no thought of drawing back.

His hands lifted to gently curve the lightly padded bones at her shoulders, and he leaned forward, brushing his mouth across one softly perfumed cheek then the other. Then, just as she was about to take that vital step back so that she could smile at him with studied indifference, he outmanoeuvred her, holding her firmly in front of him, eyes flashing wickedly just before his mouth came to cover hers in a hot and hungry kiss which took no account of how public he was being, or how blithely he had overstepped the invisible line she had drawn between them four years ago.

It took several long, turbulent seconds for her to realise just what he was doing, but by then it was too late; shock had already sent her arching into the familiar hardness of his body, and her mouth—parting on a gasp of surprise—was suddenly consumed by the feel and taste of him, remembering, and she quivered, the sheer horror of what was happening sending her eyes wide to stare in mute protest into the flashing triumph in his. Then his dark lashes were lowering sensually over his eyes, and he was giving himself up to the sheer pleasure of the kiss, drawing her even closer to him, forcing her to acknowledge the damning evidence of her own response when her breasts swelled and hardened, aroused by the crushing pressure of his chest.

'You have no idea how much I needed that,' he murmured with heavy satisfaction when at last he allowed their mouths to separate.

She jerked angrily away from him, dazed by the unexpected onslaught, and dizzy with the sight and sound and smell of him. She was trembling all over, and guilty heat ran up her cheeks. Guy had not affected her like this for years.

OK, she reasoned with herself as she struggled to pull herself together. So the bitterness she used to feel towards him had slowly faded, but she had never expected this—this swamp of feeling to overtake her! She slid a shaking hand across her mouth in a useless attempt to wipe away the lingering throb of his kiss, glancing up at him through her lashes with dark, angry eyes. 'God, Guy,' she whispered huskily. 'Sometimes you behave like a——'

'I do hope, *cara*,' he interrupted lazily, 'that you are not about to deny your own response to that kiss.' He quirked an eyebrow at her, daring her with the taunting mockery in his gaze to do just that. 'Nor mine to you,' he added silkily. 'For, while you bow your head in that oh, so demure way and make believe you are too *fastidious* to enjoy a kiss from me, you are also glaring in the general direction where your own twin proofs still peak in recognition of their master... You really should wear more concealing undergarments, Marnie, my love, if you do not wish to be so—exposed, as they say.'

'God, I hate you!'

'I know,' he drawled, unrepentant.

'Does it give you some kind of perverted kick to embarrass me this way?'

'Oh, it gives me all kinds of kicks to see you knocked off balance now and then.' The curt remark was accompanied by his abrupt withdrawal from her, leaving her standing alone, trying hard not to sway dizzily. The angry heat in her cheeks told him he had easily won that round. 'Come,' he said, suddenly cool and aloof. 'We have business to discuss. I have a car waiting outside.'

With that, he took her arm in a possessive hold, and, keeping her close to his side, led her towards the airport exit.

'No luggage?' he enquired a few steps further on.

She shook her head. 'I was hoping to catch the last shuttle back to London.'

'Which leaves in about—one hour,' he informed her with dry sarcasm. 'Rather optimistic of you, to believe we can talk and get back here in that time, don't you think?'

'An hour?' She stopped to stare at him in horror. It had never occurred to her to check the times of the London shuttle! She had just automatically assumed they ran day and night—the way the trains did.

'What will you do now?' Guy murmured provokingly. 'Stuck here in this strange city with a man you say you hate!'

'I'll most probably survive,' she threw back tartly, 'since the man in question can't possibly hurt me more than he has already!'

His mouth tightened, but he said nothing, pulling her along beside him as he strode through the exit doors. The waiting car was long and dark and chauffeur-driven. Guy politely saw her seated before sliding in beside her, and almost before the door had closed them in they were moving smoothly away from the kerb.

CHAPTER THREE

'I'M GOING to have to find somewhere to stay overnight,' Marnie sighed, still irritated because she had been so stupid as to not check the times of the return shuttle back to London. A couple of hours of Guy's company was all she ever allowed herself at one swallow. The mere idea of spending a whole evening in his proximity was enough to make her voice sound pettish as she added, 'And I'm hungry; I missed my lunch today and you——' '

'Do be quiet, Marnie,' Guy cut in, sending her a look of such flat derision that her cheeks actually flushed at it. 'You know as well as I do that I will have made any necessary arrangements. I am nothing if not competent, Marnie—nothing if not that...'

She glared at him balefully, hating him with her eyes for his ever-present sarcasm. Oh, yes, she agreed, Guy was competent, all right. So competent, in fact, that it had taken her almost a year to find out that he was cheating on her with another woman. And she would not have found out then if Jamie hadn't opened his mouth over something he'd thought completely innocent at the time.

Jamie. She shivered suddenly. God, how Guy hated her brother for that bit of indiscretion. He had vowed once never to forgive him. Just as she had vowed never to forgive Guy.

'Cold?' he murmured, noting the small shiver.

'No.' She shook her head. 'Just...' Her lips closed over what she had been going to say, and she turned her face away from him with a small non-committal shrug. She could feel the sharpness of his gaze on her and tensed slightly, waiting for him to prompt her into finishing the sentence. The silence between them grew fraught, shortening her breathing and making her heart beat faster. There was so much bitterness between them, so much dissension, she didn't know whether she could actually go through with this.

'Easy, Marnie...' Guy's hand reached out to cover her own, and it was only as the warm brown fingers closed gently over hers that she realised she was sitting with her hands locked into a white-knuckled clench. 'It cannot be this bad, surely?' he murmured huskily.

Oh, yes, it could, she thought silently. I hate you and you hate Jamie and Jamie hates himself. It couldn't be much worse! 'Guy,' she began tentatively, 'about Jamie...'

'No.' He removed his hand, and at the same time removed the caring expression from his face. And Marnie felt her heart sink as he leaned back and closed his eyes, effectively shutting her out. It was an old habit of his, and one she knew well. If Guy wished to defer a discussion he simply gave you no room to speak. On a soft sigh, she subsided, accepting that it was no use her trying to force the issue. Even if she tried, he would completely ignore her. It was the way of the man, hard, stubborn, despotic to a certain extent. He played at life by his own set of rules and principles and never allowed anyone to dictate to him.

Besides his undeniably fantastic looks, Guy was a brilliant businessman, a wildly exciting athlete and a dynamic lover. True to his Latin blood, he possessed charm in abundance, arrogance by the ton, energy enough to satisfy six women, and money enough to keep them all in luxury while he did so.

It was that same surfeit of money in the family which gave him the means to indulge his second most favourite passion: that for racing cars. It was a passion that had taken him all over the world to race, living the kind of life that automatically went along with it, his striking good looks and innate charm making sexual conquests so easy for him that by the time he met her Guy had grown cynical beyond belief about the opposite sex.

He had just passed his thirty-fourth birthday by then, and retired from racing on a blaze of glory by winning his second world championship crown, to take up the reins of business from his father 'so the old man can go and tend to his roses,' as Guy so drolly liked to put it.

Papa Frabosa...a small frown pulled at her smooth brow. It was ages since she'd seen him. And not because of her break-up with his son, she reminded herself grimly. No, not even that had been able to break the loving bond she and Roberto had forged during her short foray into their lives. But he liked to keep to his Berkshire home these days, since the small stroke several months ago, and Marnie had refused to so much as set foot on the estate since she'd left Guy. The place resurrected too many painful memories.

Opening her mouth to ask him about how his father was, she turned her head to look at him—and immediately forgot all about Roberto Frabosa when she found herself gazing at Guy's lean, dark profile.

Such a beautiful man, she observed with an ache. A man with everything going for him. Too much for her to cope with. That dynamic character of his needed far more stimulation than an ordinary little artist girl had been able to offer him. She was at least ten years too young for him, ten years behind him in experience—a lesson she had learned the hard way, and had no desire to repeat even though she knew without a single doubt that if she said to him right now, and with no prior warning, that she wanted to be his wife again, Guy would take her back without question. He loved her in his own way, with passion and with spirit. But not in the way she needed to be loved—faithfully. His need to supplement his physical desires with other women had driven a stake so deeply into her heart that the wound still bled profusely—four years on.

He didn't know, of course, just how deeply he had hurt her. He only knew the small amount she had allowed him to know—and to be fair to him he had never forgiven himself for hurting her that much. His sense of remorse and the knowledge that he had no defence for his behaviour had kept him coming back to her throughout the years in the bleak hope that she might one day learn to forgive him and perhaps take him back. He was a Catholic by religion, and, although they had not married in the Catholic faith, and their divorce had been quite legal, Guy had never accepted it as so. 'One life, one wife' was his motto, and she was it. Guy had refused to melt out of her life, and with his usual stubbornness had refused to let her do the melting. So they'd gone on over the years, sharing a strange kind of relationship that hovered somewhere between very close friends and bitter adversaries. He lived in hope that one day she might find it in her to forgive him, and she lived in the hope that one day she would force him to accept that she would not—which was why she did all the bitter biting, and he allowed her to get away with it.

A penance, he'd described it once. A penance for his sins, like the four years they had spent apart. He quite readily accepted it all as deserved. 'You'll forgive me one day, Marnie,' he told her once when one of his many seduction scenes had been foiled—by the skin of her chattering teeth! 'I will allow you some more time—but not much more,' he'd warned. 'Because time is slowly running out for both of us. Papa wants to hold his grandson in his arms before he dies, and I mean to see that he does.'

'Then don't look to me to provide it!' she flashed with enough bitter venom to whiten his face. 'You would do better, Guy, finding yourself the kind of wife who doesn't mind sharing you, because this one has no intention of going through that kind of hell again!'

'And I have already vowed to you that it would not happen again!' he said haughtily. Guy always became haughty when on the defensive; he hated it so much. 'That one time was a mistake, one which——'

'One which was more than enough for me!' she'd cut him off before he'd got started—as she always did when he tried to explain. 'Why can't you get it into your thick head that I don't love you any more?' she'd added ruthlessly, yet felt no satisfaction in the way his expression had closed her out, the flicker of pain she'd glimpsed in him managing only to hurt her too.

That was all of five months ago, and since then she'd steered well clear of Guy. But now here she was, driving with him through the streets of Edinburgh knowing with a dull sinking feeling inside that this time he held all the cards, and she had nothing but her pride—if he allowed her to keep it, that was, which was no real certainty.

'We have arrived,' his quiet voice broke into her thoughts, and she turned to glance at the porticoed entrance to one of the city's most exclusive hotels.

He helped her alight, as always the complete gentleman in public, his hand lightly cupping her elbow as they walked inside and led the way to the waiting lift. Neither of them spoke a single word; neither of them felt inclined to. It was the calm before the storm, with both of them conserving their energies for what they knew was to come.

The lift doors closed then opened again several seconds later. Guy guided her out on to the quiet landing and towards a pair of rather imposing white-painted doors, a key dangling casually from his fingers.

She shuddered—she couldn't help it—and he glanced sharply at her, his mouth tightening into a stubborn line because he knew exactly what she was thinking, and his fingers tightened on her arm as if in confirmation of her fear that this time—this time there would be no compromises, no escape for her.

The suite was more a mini-apartment, with several doors leading off from a small hallway. Guy pushed open one of the doors and indicated that she should precede him into a large and luxuriously furnished sitting-room.

'Nice,' she drawled, impressed.

'Adequate,' dismissed the man who had spent most of his life living out of a suitcase. He possessed a real contempt of hotels now. He much preferred his rambling country home in Berkshire, or his beautiful apartment in London. 'Sit down and I'll mix us both a drink,' he invited.

Moving with the lean grace Marnie always associated with him, Guy went over to the small bar and began opening cupboard doors while she hovered for a moment, wondering on a sudden swell of panic if she should just turn right around and get out of here while she still could.

Then she remembered Jamie's bruised and swollen face, and that linen sling around his broken arm. And she remembered Clare, and the desire to run and save her own skin faded away.

For Clare's peace of mind it was worth it, she told herself as a memory so painful that it clenched at her chest struck her. Stress was a dangerous state of mind—could even kill if left to run wild. She would do almost anything to ensure her sister-in-law never had to experience it.

With a grim setting of her lips, she moved across the room and sat down in one of the soft-cushioned armchairs.

'Here.' Guy handed her a tall glass filled almost to the rim with a clear sparkling liquid. 'Dry martini with lots of soda,' he informed her, going to sit in the other chair while she smiled wryly at the sardonic tone he had used. It had always amused him that she disliked the taste of alcohol in any form. A dry martini well watered down was just about her limit.

The ice cubes clinked against the side of the glass as Guy took a sip at his own gin and tonic. Then, 'OK, Marnie,' he said briskly. 'Let me have it. What's that stupid brother of yours done now that could make you come to me for help?'

'How do you know it's Jamie who needs your help?' she flashed indignantly, annoyed that he wasn't even giving her a chance to work up to mentioning Jamie, and forgetting that she had already given him a clue in the car. 'I could be here on my own behalf, you know, but typical of you: you immediately jump to your own conclusions and——'

'*Are* you here for your own sake?' he cut in smoothly.

'No...' Marnie wriggled uncomfortably where she sat. 'But you could at least give me a chance to explain before you——'

'Then it has to be for Jamie,' he said, ignoring her indignation. 'I warned you, Marnie,' he inserted grimly, ignoring all the rest, 'not to bring your brother's troubles to me again, and I meant it.'

'This time it's different, though,' she told him, her mouth thin and tight because, no matter how sure she was that she was doing the right thing, she didn't have to like it, 'or I wouldn't have involved you at all, but this time it's Clare I'm worried about, and...'

'Clare?' he repeated sharply. His eyes suddenly narrowed and went hard. 'What's he done to her?' he demanded harshly.

'Nothing!' Marnie denied, resenting his condemning tone. 'He worships the ground she walks on and you know it. Of course Jamie hasn't done anything to hurt Clare—how could you even think such a thing?'

'I worshipped the ground you walked on and look how badly I hurt you,' he pointed out.

'No, you didn't,' she denied that deridingly. 'You worshipped my body, and when it wasn't available for you you just went out and found a substitute for it. So don't you dare try putting Jamie into the same selfish mould as you exist in! He *loves* Clare,' she stated tightly, 'loves as in lifelong caring and fidelity—something you've never felt for anyone in your whole life!'

'Finished?' he clipped.

'Yes.' She subsided at the angry glint now glowing in his narrowed eyes.

'Then if Jamie is this—caring of Clare, why have you been forced to come to me to beg help for her?'

'Because . . .' She sucked in a deep breath, trying to get a grasp on her growling temper. He could always do it. One minute in his company and he could always rile her until she didn't know what she was saying! 'She's pregnant,' she said.

'What—already?' Guy made a sound of grinding impatience. 'I don't call that damned caring of your brother, Marnie,' he muttered angrily. 'I call it downright irresponsible!'

So do I, she thought, but held the words back. Guy didn't need any help in finding faults with her brother. He had an unerring ability to just pluck them out of the air like rabbits from a magician's hat!

'What's the matter with her?' he went on grimly. 'Is she ill—does she need money for medical care?'

Already he was fishing inside jacket pocket for his cheque-book, his glass discarded so he could write out a cheque for whatever amount Marnie wished to demand from him.

And she was tempted—oh, so severely tempted to just let it go at that and name a figure which would probably choke him at the size of it but would not stop him giving it to her because it was for little Clare, whom he'd always had a soft spot for and therefore would do anything for.

But that would not be right—nor fair, she acknowledged heavily. If he was going to help them out, then he had a right to know the truth.

'Wait a mintue,' she said, swallowing because the truth was going to be that much harder to tell now he'd all but convinced himself Clare was in dire need of his financial asistance. 'You haven't heard it all, and I would rather you did before you agreed to anything. Clare is pregnant, but not in any danger of losing this one just yet, though it is the fear that it may happen which made me come to you.'

'Jamie,' he said, sitting back, the cheque-book thrown contemptuously aside.

She nodded, deciding it was time to stop prevaricating. He deserved that after the way he had reacted to the thought of Clare's needing his help. It even warmed her to know that Guy could be so generous to someone he barely knew.

'He's just completed the reconstruction of a 1955 Jaguar XK 140 Drophead,' she began.

'I have one of those!' Guy's mood instantly changed to one of glowing enthusiasm. 'I wonder if he managed to solve the problem with the——?'

'While he was delivering it to the owner yesterday...' she interrupted him a trifle impatiently; it was typical of him to be so easily diverted by the name of a precious car '... a lorry coming in the other direction skidded on a patch of oil and ploughed straight into him. The Jaguar was written off.'

'What—totally?' He was horrifed.

'It went up in flames,' she informed him grimly.

'Bloody stupid—anyone seriously hurt?'

'In general, my brother lives a charmed life,' Marnie sighed. 'No, not seriously,' she confirmed. 'Jamie managed to climb out of the tangled mess just before it caught fire with nothing more than a bruised face and a broken arm for his trouble.'

'That beaufiful car,' Guy murmured in the mournful tone of the true car fanatic. 'Jamie must be sick.'

'You could say that,' Marnie agreed. 'The car wasn't insured.'

That dragged Guy surely back on course. He stared at her in blank amazement, then looked appalled, then just downright disgusted. 'How much?' he snapped.

She told him, he swore loudly and she grimaced, entirely in sympathy with him.

'And I suppose he's hoping that good old Guy will come up with the readies to bail him out.' His tone was scathing to say the least. 'Well, you can just go back and tell him that it's no go this time, Marnie! I have just about had enough of that reckless brother of yours and his stupid——'

'You've missed the point,' she put in quietly, catching his attention before his Italian temperament ran away with him.

'What point?' he demanded.

'Clare,' she reminded him.

'Clare?' Guy looked blank for a moment, then went as pale as a ghost. 'She wasn't in the car with him, was she?' he choked.

'No!' Marnie quickly assured him. 'No—that wasn't the point I was trying to make. But—Guy,' she appealed to him for understanding, 'she's pregnant and she shouldn't be! It was already a big enough shock for her to have Jamie come home with his face all bruised and his arm in a sling—how do you think she's going to react when she finds out she forgot to renew his insurance policy and that they've now got to find upwards of fifty thousand pounds to compensate the owner of the car?'

Silence. Guy was staring at her through hard, angry eyes as he let all of it really sink in, and Marnie sat there staring back with her lovely blue eyes wide in anxious appeal, hoping that just this once—this one last time—he would come up trumps for her and help them out without demanding anything back in return.

'He promises to pay you back—Guy,' she added quickly, when he continued to say nothing, 'he—he said to tell you he's managed to acquire an MG K3 Magnette and you can have that as a down-payment. And he's——'

'A damned fool if he thinks I would accept anything from him!' Guy cut in impatiently. 'And I warned you, Marnie, quite distinctly, the last time you came begging to me on his behalf, that I had done more than enough for the man who wrecked our marriage,' he reminded her forcefully.

'Jamie didn't wreck our marriage,' she said wearily. 'You did that all on your own.'

The dark head shook grimly. 'We would still be together,' stated the man who had always preferred to scatter blame around like raindrops so long as none of it stuck to himself, 'living together—loving together, if your stupid brother hadn't stuck his nose into my affairs.'

'"Affairs" being the operative word,' she derided.

'Damn you, Marnie!' Angrily, he climbed out of his chair, frustration making him run a hand through the thick, sleek blackness of his hair. 'I didn't mean it in that way—and you know it!' He turned to glare down at her, then sucked in a deep, calming breath. 'Your brother was directly responsible for——'

'I don't want to discuss it.' It was her turn to cut him short—as she always did when he attempted to bring up the past. 'It's all just dead news now.'

'Not while I'm still breathing, it is not,' he bit out. 'We still have unfinished business, you and I,' he went on to warn, wagging a long finger at her in a way which was consciously gauged to infuriate her. 'And, until you are prepared to give me a fair hearing, it will remain unfinished. Just remember that as you sit there hating me with your beautiful eyes. For one day I will make you listen, and then it will be you doing the apologising and I taking revenge!'

'Oh, yes.' The scorn in her voice derided him outright. 'As I think I've already said, I don't want to talk about it. I came here today to——'

'Beg for more money for your useless brother,' Guy tartly supplied for her.

'No,' she angrily denied that. 'To beg for Clare!' She too came to her feet, irritation and frustration in every line of her slender frame. 'I was as determined as you are not to bail Jamie out of any more of his disasters,' she snapped. 'I told him this time and in no uncertain terms that I would not involve you again! But—God,' she sighed, lifting her strained eyes to his, 'this is different, Guy, you've got to see that? This time it isn't just you and me and Jamie we're fighting about; it involves Clare! Sweet, gentle Clare who has never wished harm on anyone in her entire life! You can't turn your back on her, Guy, surely? Not just to gain your sweet revenge over Jamie?'

He was going to refuse, she could see it in the grim, hard cut of his tightly held mouth, and panic began to shimmer inside her. 'Please, Guy.' She lifted a trembling hand to clutch pleadingly at the bunching muscles in his upper arm. 'Please . . .' she begged.

He looked long and hard into the deep blue of her pleading eyes, his own so dark and disturbing that Marnie's insides began to churn with an old memory so sweet and aching that she wanted to cry out against it. Once she had drowned in that look, placed all her vulnerable love and trust in its meaning what it appeared to tell her.

She watched him glance down to where her hand clutched at him, his beautiful eyelashes forming a thick, sweeping arch against his strong cheekbones. Watched the hardness ease from his mouth as he lifted his gaze back to her own, and suddenly the silence between them began to throb with tension—a raw sexual tension that had no right to show itself at this vital moment! Marnie moved, her tingling fingers flexing slightly in an effort to dispel the unwanted sensation, her tongue flicking in agitation across the fullness of her suddenly dry lips, her breathing slow and heavy.

Guy saw it all, every revealing thing she was experiencing at this new kind of physical closeness, and something unfathomable passed across his face... a further darkening of those rich brown eyes that had her holding her breath in dear hope that her plea was reaching him.

'Please...' she repeated huskily. 'Put your prejudices aside this one last time—for Clare's sake?'

He hesitated visibly—long enough to make hope flare into her eyes—only to have him dip his dark head a little closer to her own as he countered softly but with a ruthlessness that left her in no doubt at all to his meaning, 'And you, Marnie? Are you prepared to put your own prejudices aside, for sweet Clare's sake?'

Her thudding heart sank, her body went cold, and she stood very still, staring into the utterly uncompromising set of his lean, dark features, wondering why she had actually had the gall to convince herself that she could win him round this one last time. Guy had, after all, told her in no uncertain terms not to come begging to him again unless she was prepared to pay the price. She had never known him say anything without carrying it through. It was what made him the man he was today, this stubborn unwillingness of his to compromise over anything—even the way he conducted his life, she reminded herself grimly. Married or not, Guy had always refused to answer to anyone but himself.

Unclipping her hand from his arm, she took a shaky step back from him, then turned away so she wouldn't have to witness the flare of triumph her answer would put in his eyes. 'Yes,' she whispered, 'I'm prepared to do that.'

Oddly, and surprisingly since she had just conceded to him what he had been trying to get her to do for four long years now, instead of thrusting his triumph down her throat, Guy too turned away, going to stand over by the window.

'How prepared?' he persisted, not turning to face her with the final challenge, his back a rigid bulk of taut muscle for her to stare bleakly upon.

'Whatever it takes,' she promised flatly. 'Whatever it is you want in return.'

'You.' He turned his head, his expression as cool and uncompromising as she had ever known it. 'I want you back.'

She had expected it. Had travelled up here knowing exactly what he would demand; so why did she experience the sudden drain of blood from her head, or the blow of pain that knocked all the breath from her body in a way that sent her sinking down on to the sofa? 'Oh, God, Guy,' she whispered threadily, 'I don't think I can!'

If she thought him remote before, then her broken little cry managed to close him up completely, seeming to rake over every nerve-end he possessed before turning him into a cold statue of ungiving rock.

'I did warn you not to involve me in your brother's problems again,' he said harshly. 'I also remember warning you that my—penance for hurting you had almost run its course.' He let out a sharp sigh as he watched her wrap her arms tightly around her trembling body as if she was protecting herself from his very words. 'It is time to break this—foolish deadlock we are both stuck in, Marnie!'

'But I don't belong to you any more!' she cried.

'You have always belonged to me!' he snapped, moving at last to come and stand over her, his anger so palpable that she could actually feel it throbbing out of him. 'All you have done here today is save me the trouble of finding my own way to get you back!'

'By using Jamie?' she jeered. 'Using the weak to aid the strong?'

Guy nodded curtly, taking no offence at the accusation. 'Just as Jamie uses your strength to prop up his own weaknesses, Marnie. It works both ways, my dear.'

'And Clare?' she demanded.

'Clare is your weakness, Marnie,' Guy stated. 'Not mine. Not even Jamie's. I wonder why that is?'

Marnie looked away from the probing thrust of his hard black eyes, not willing—never willing to confess just why she held such a vulnerable spot in her heart for her sister-in-law.

'So, in what capacity am I to become your property this time, Guy?' she enquired bitterly, finally conceding the point that she was indeed entirely in his power. She lifted her gaze to show him an ice-cold contempt that held his own face taut and grim. 'Wife or mistress?' she posed. 'Not that one has any precedence over the other in your life,' she acknowledged cynically, 'but your father will condone nothing less than a legal marriage between us, you must already know that.'

'Then for my father's sake, of course——' he shrugged as if it mattered little to him either way '—we will be man and wife again—not that I have considered us anything less during the last four years,' he added drily.

Marnie's mouth took on a contemptuous line. 'If we're to take into consideration your behaviour over the last four years as well as the one we were actually married, Guy, then the adultery charge can be laid at your feet a dozen times over.' Her eyes leapt to spit accusation at him. 'Or is it two dozen—or four?'

'Bitch!' he growled, reaching down to grasp hold of her. 'That is for me to know and you to wonder about! A wife's place is at her husband's side, warming his bed and keeping his body content! Your desertion of those duties leaves you with no right to question how I quenched my needs, and nor ever will it in the future!'

'I see,' she sneered, 'then what is good for the goose is most definitely good enough for the gander—remember that, Mr God's-Gift-to-Women Frabosa, when you carry on your little affairs. I may be back in your power again, but only for as long as it takes me to prove what a worthless rat you really are!'

'Be careful what you say to me, Marnie!' he warned, the anger vibrating from every pore as he took hold of her shoulders in a rough grip. 'I have taken the bitterness from your vicious tongue for long enough—paid for my crimes a thousand times over, and will pay no longer!'

Flushed and trembling with hurts which went back years, and quivering with a hated, hot searing sense of awareness at his physical closeness, Marnie glared at him with contempt. 'So get thee behind me, woman!' she scorned his arrogance. 'For I am your lord and master!'

'Yes!' he hissed, almost lifting her out of the chair with the hard grasp of his hands. 'That is exactly it! Now stop riling me to anger.' He threw her away from him, to straighten up. 'And accept the inevitable with the kind of grace I know you to possess. It is over, at last and with deep relief on my part. You and I are as one from this moment on and I will hear no more of your malice—understand?'

She understood only too well, sliding from anger to depression with a speed that spoke volumes about her defeat.

He remained standing over her for a long time, staring down at her bent head until her nerves began to fray beneath the tension she was putting on them. Then, with a sigh which came from somewhere deep and dark inside him, he moved away, slamming out of the door without another word.

CHAPTER FOUR

SIGHING, Marnie let her head sink back into the soft-cushioned sofa and closed her eyes.

So, she thought heavily. After four years of relative peace and contentment, she was back with a man who could only make her life hell for a second time. Living with Guy the first time had been no picnic. He possessed too volatile a temperament to make him a comfortable person to be around. And she was just too spirited to be anything but a spark to his fire. The only place they had ever found any mutual accord had been in bed, and even that had proved itself inadequate in the end.

Did he believe that forcing her to come back to him would automatically heal all that had gone before? she wondered cynically. Or was it just that he did not care so long as he had her back where he considered she belonged. He possessed a colossal pride, and she had dented it badly when she walked out on him. Having her back would mend that dent, show him to be the irresistible Guy Frabosa everyone always thought him to be.

He came back into the room, and Marnie stirred herself enough to stand up. 'I need to use the bathroom,' she said coolly.

'Of course.' His dark head dipped, a new stiffness entering the atmosphere now the main battle was over. He opened the sitting-room door again and waited for her to precede him out of it, then indicated another door in the tiny hall. A bedroom, she discovered as she stepped inside. 'There is a bathroom *en suite* through that door opposite.' He informed her. 'While you freshen up, I shall go and order us something to eat.' With another nod he was gone, closing the door behind him on Marnie's wretched sigh of relief.

When she came back to the sitting-room Guy was talking on the telephone, his tone that brisk, clipped, arrogant one he used when issuing orders to his minions; she smiled at it, hoping it was that frosty-voiced woman she had come up against earlier. It gave her a real sense of satisfaction to know that that was one tone of voice Guy had never used with her—thank God, because it sent ice-cold shivers up and down her spine just listening to it.

He hadn't noticed her return, his dark head bowed to study the shiny leather of his hand-made shoes as he leaned against the edge of the huge desk which had always been an essential requisite for any hotel room he stayed in. And she paused on the threshold of the room, the artist in her drawn to follow the long, lean length of him.

He hadn't altered much in the last five years, she noted wryly, sliding her eyes along the full length of his powerful legs encased in their usual expensive silk-wool mix with creases so sharp, they accentuated the flatness of his taut, narrow hips.

She had once painted Guy in many guises. The dynamic racing-car driver decked out in a silver space-suit, his head lost beneath a big crash helmet which left only his eyes, gleaming out from the gap where the protective plastic visor would be flicked into place the moment he climbed behind the wheel. But, while he waited, those eyes would spark and glitter with all the fevered impatience for what he was about to take on. Then there was the mocking painting she'd done of him when he looked like a sloth, lazily stretched out in an armchair wearing nothing more than a loosely tied robe about his naked body, hair ruffled and his square chin roughened by a twelve-hour shadow, attention fixed on the Sunday newspaper like any ordinary mortal man. As studies, they were almost ridiculous in their stark contrast to each other, yet both held a kind of magic that could set a thrill of excitement tingling up and down her spine, because nothing could ever disguise the latent power of the man himself. Not the all-encompassing space-suit or the unkempt sloth—or even this elegantly clad, super-dynamic tycoon she was looking at now, she added as her eyes lifted to take in the muscled beauty of his torso beneath the crisp white shirt he was wearing. In every persona, Guy always managed to exude what was the sheer male essence of the man—that hot, pulsing core of raw sexuality which could still make her body react violently, even while her heart remained coldly unimpressed.

He muttered something, and her eyes flicked up to clash with his, heat crawling up her cheeks because he had caught her staring so blatantly at him. She stiffened slightly, her chin coming up in defiance of the expression he had managed to catch on her face before she blanked it out, but his own eyes mocked her as they stared back, his hand slow in setting the telephone receiver back on its rest.

Damn his sex appeal! she thought as the tension began whipping itself up between them. Damn him for thrusting his sexuality at her! And damn herself for responding to it.

'I—I forgot to fetch my bag,' she said, forcibly dragging her eyes away from him to send them on a slightly hazy search of the luxurious lounge. 'Did you see where I put it when I came in?' She was too busy refusing to let her eyes be drawn back to him to see the sudden narrowing of his eyes. 'I'm sure I dropped it down here,' she murmured, walking over to the sofa to frown down at the place she'd expected the bag to be.

'What do you need it for?' he asked.

'My comb.' Her hand jerked nervously up to her where her hair, newly released from its severe style, hung in thick silk tendrils down her back. 'I'd let it down before I realised I hadn't got my comb.'

'Here.' She glanced at him, expecting to find her bag dangling from his outstretched fingers, but frowned when all he held was his own tortoiseshell comb.

'No, thank you,' she primly refused, and returned to searching for her bag. 'I have my own somewhere if I could lay my hands on my...'

It hit her then, why he was standing there looking so studiedly casual, and she turned back to glare at him. 'You've got it!' she accused, her hands going to rest on her hips in an unconsciously shrewish pose.

He took his time enjoying the highly provocative stance, an aggravating smile playing about his lips as he slid his gaze along the figure-hugging purple dress which did little to hide the sensual curves in her body or the too expressive heave of her full breasts. 'Have you any idea what you look like standing there like that?' he drawled.

'A mess, most likely,' she dismissed the husky tease in his voice. 'My bag, Guy,' she clipped. 'You've moved it and I want it.' A slender hand came out in demand.

Guy glanced at it then back at her face, then, still smiling lazily, he gave a slow shake of his head. 'No,' he said. 'I'm sorry *cara*, but until you are legally tied to me once again, you will need nothing that is in that bag.'

'What's that supposed to mean?' she asked in genuine bewilderment.

'Exactly what it said,' he drawled. 'For the next few days you will be making not a single move without me at your side. Anything you may require will be provided by me, including a comb for your lovely hair.'

'But Guy,' she protested in disbelief, 'that's——'

'Not up for discussion,' he inserted, straightening from the desk to begin walking towards her, his tortoiseshell comb held out once again. 'I do not trust you, Marnie, to keep your part of our bargain,' he informed her bluntly. 'And, since my part has already been attended to while you were out of the room, I feel the need of some assurance that you will not cheat me. Here, take the comb.' He thrust it at her, and Marnie took it simply because he gave her no choice.

'But this is ridiculous!' she choked. 'Guy, I have no intention of cheating you! Stop being so childish and hand over my bag,' she demanded. 'There are other things I need from it beside a damned comb!'

'A lipstick, perhaps? I prefer your mouth exactly as it is, soft and pulsing with its own natural colour.' Arrogantly he reached up to rub the pad of his thumb against her bottom lip, and instantly the blood began to pump into the sensitive flesh, filling it out and bringing a blaze of fury to her eyes as she angrily slapped him away. 'Or maybe you want your neat stack of credit cards,' he continued unperturbed. 'Or the wallet of paper money which would easily get you a ride out of here.'

'But I have no intention of going anywhere!' she cried in exasperation.

'And I have no intention of giving you the chance,' he agreed. 'So drop the outrage,' he ordered coolly. 'You know me well enough to know that I always learn by my mistakes. Disappearing is something you do too well for my peace of mind. So I have taken the necessary precautions to make sure you cannot.'

Wilting on a wave of defeat, she sank down on to the cushioned arm of the sofa and sighed, his last remarks cooling her temper more than anything else could have done. Four years ago he had trusted her to stay put in Berkshire where he had left her, stupidly believing the move from London to his country home was a sensible way of giving her time to get over her understandable aversion to him. She stayed put only long enough to watch him drive away, then, while his father had believed her safely ensconced in her room, she had left, taking nothing with her but the clothes she stood up in and her bag containing enough money to get her as far away from Guy's influence as she could get.

She had ended up in a tiny village in the Fens, where she had succeeded in hiding herself away for six long, wretched months before she'd felt fit to face the world—and Guy again.

No, she conceded heavily, Guy was not a man to make the same mistake twice. There was no way he would give her the opportunity to repeat that particular trick.

A knock at the outer suite door broke the sudden heavy silence throbbing in the air between them. Guy hesitated, looking as if he was going to say something, then sighed and turned away, walking with a smooth animal grace out of the room.

He came back wheeling a dinner-trolley in front of him, his expression hooded as he glanced across to where Marnie still sat, staring blankly at some indefinable spot on the carpet.

'Come and eat,' he said gruffly.

Marnie gave a small shake of her head in an effort to re-focus her thoughts, then came to her feet. 'I want to tidy my hair first,' she said, and left the room before Guy could glimpse the pain her short flight into the past had put into her eyes.

Five minutes later, her hair and her composure restored to something closer to their usual smoothness, she turned her attention for the first time on the room she was standing in, and forced herself to consider what Guy's intentions regarding their sleeping arrangements would be. The room was furnished in classical tones: Wedgwood blue and neutral beige, the big double bed the one piece of furniture which dominated the room.

Signs—unnervingly familiar signs—of Guy's habitation of the room were scattered about. His black silk robe, thrown negligently over a chair. A white shirt he must have discarded for a clean one before coming to meet her at the airport tossed upon the bed. And a stack of small change, thrown negligently on to the bedside table and forgotten about as had always been his way. He held a real contempt of the sound of small change jingling in his pocket and tended to discard it the first chance he could get, so she would save it all up in a big coffee-jar, then carefully count it out and bag it before taking it to her favourite charity, more respectful of money, having never been used to having it, than he would ever be. It had amused him, to watch her hoarding his cast-off money like that, and she had glared defiantly at him. 'You can stand there and laugh,' she'd snapped once. 'But do you realise that you've managed to discard one hundred and ninety-five pounds in small change this month? It's a good job the Salvation Army aren't so picky,' she'd grumbled. 'They're not too proud to have it jingle in their pockets!'

'So, they should be grateful that I dislike it jingling in mine so much,' dismissed a man who refused to be anything but amused at her contempt.

Marnie smiled to herself, going over to sift with an idle finger through the small heap. Five pound coins at a glance, she gauged ruefully. Shame she wasn't around any longer to bag it for the Salvation Army.

But she was around, she remembered on a small shiver. Back in Guy's orbit and destined to stay this time. Her stomach knotted, catching at her breath as she turned to scan the elegant room.

Would he expect her to sleep here with him tonight? Her gaze settled on his dark silk robe, and almost instantly she conjured up a vision of him throwing it there, his body smooth and tight and disturbingly graceful in its nakedness. No pyjamas to be seen. She knew without having to look that she could turn this room upside-down without finding any. Guy never wore anything in bed. 'Except you,' he'd grinned once when she had dared ask the question. 'You are all I need to keep me warm.'

God. Her chest lifted and fell on a thickened heave of air. She just couldn't do it—couldn't! Not just calmly go to bed with him tonight as if nothing untoward had occurred in the last four years!

Shifting jerkily, she sent that damning bed one last pensive glance before she walked out of the room and stood, hovering in the hallway, small teeth pressing down on her trembling bottom lip as she glanced at the other couple of doors which led off from here.

More bedrooms? Her heart thudded with hope, and she stepped over to open the one next to Guy's, almost wilting in relief when she saw it was indeed another bedroom.

Perhaps, she mused thoughtfully as she quietly closed the door again, if she played it very carefully, this would be the room she'd sleep in tonight—alone. She knew Guy, knew his strengths and his weaknesses. With a little clever manipulation on her part, she should be able to swing things to suit herself.

'What are you doing?' His voice made her jump, and swing around to find him standing in the sitting-room doorway.

'Checking out my prision,' she countered. 'Why, have you some objection to my doing that as well?' Her tone was a challenge as well as a defiance to his power over her.

'No, no objection,' he assured, leaning his shoulder against the open door and thrusting his hands into his pockets as he studied her narrowly. 'So, what have you discovered—besides the fact that I have no "little fancy piece" hidden away in one of the other rooms?' he mocked.

The thought having never entered her head, Marnie was instantly on the attack at being reminded of his—habit of travelling nowhere without the necessary woman in tow.

'So, where is she, then?' she demanded. 'Perhaps occupying the suite next door?'

'Wherever she is, she will sleep alone tonight.' His dismissive shrug was both lazy and indifferent, but his eyes held a promise that left Marnie in no doubt why this faceless creature would be alone.

Quelling the urge to tell him that he too was in for a disappointment, she kept balefully silent instead.

He wasn't sure what was going on behind the look, but experience warned him that something was, and he continued to study her narrowly for a few tense seconds before letting out a dry little sigh and levering himself away from the door.

'Dinner's getting cold,' he murmured.

'Is it?' she said. 'Then we'd better go and eat it, hadn't we?' And in a complete turnabout of mood she sent him a bright smile as she walked past him. 'What did you order?' she asked as she went over to the heated serving trolley to begin lifting covers curiously. 'Mmm,' she drooled, 'is that freshwater bream? Oh, you darling, Guy, I haven't eaten freshwater bream in years! Fancy you remembering how much I love it! What's for starters?' she asked eagerly, lifting covers and peering inside with an outward ignorance of the frowning suspicion written on his face. 'Melon. Great!' She sat herself down at the table. 'If there is one thing for which I could never fault you, Guy,' she enthused, 'it was your unerring ability to always know exactly what to order for me.'

With a flick of her freshly combed hair, she sent him a wide, warm smile, wanting to laugh at his comical expression. Guy had always had difficulty following her quickfire changes of mood. He had never been certain of what she was really thinking or feeling at any one time. The fifteen years that separated their ages had their advantages on both sides, and for Marnie it meant she was like a completely new species of woman to a man of his sophistication. It had always puzzled her as to why he should turn his practised eye on someone so young and obviously unsophisticated as herself. In the end she had decided it must be the Italian in him, demanding an untouched woman for his wife, and finding innocent virgins of a more mature and sophisticated age was well nigh an impossibility these days. So once she had decided that her innocence was her only attraction she had gone into emotional hiding, treating him to a clever blend of light-hearted affection and flirtatious mockery that kept him constantly unsure of her.

Marnie had never considered herself a fool. Her mother had died when she was only sixteen, leaving her and Jamie to cope alone in the big bad world outside. But, although Jamie was several years older than Marnie, he had never been a strength for her to rely on, and she had had to learn quickly to fend for herself. Sheer guts and determination had taken her through her final few years at school and on to art college. She had paid her own way by working seven nights a week as a waitress in a wine-bar, learning very early on how to deflect any male interest in her without once feeling the urge to experiment with what they were offering her. She was willing to paint anything and everything that brought her a fee for doing it, and by the time she was in her second college year had already built a reputation for herself as an artist—nothing spectacular, but good enough to have the small commissions coming in on a regular basis. By her twentieth birthday she had had her own small flat, run her own small car—with a lot of nursing from her brother—and had already found it necessary to resign from college so she could meet her growing commitments, her career seeming to create itself out of nothing for her.

No. Nobody's fool but Guy's, she concluded. Falling in love with him had to go down as the biggest piece of folly she had ever committed in her short, busy life! Not that she had ever let him know how completely he had beguiled her. And anyway, she had fought it, fought her feelings all the way through their short, hot, volcanic courtship and right into their equally short, hot and volcanic marriage.

She'd decided that he wanted a virgin for a wife and a woman he had trained to his own personal sexual satisfaction in his bed, which was exactly what he got—and nothing else. While she got—well, what she deserved, she wryly supposed. A man who gave her everything from fine clothes and fast cars to long, hot, passionate nights that left her replete but spent, having had to fight the urge to tell him just how wretchedly she loved him.

But that was a long time ago, she concluded as she glanced up to catch him still watching her narrowly and smiled a bright, false, capricious smile which made his own mouth turn down into a scowl. Now, even the love was dead, choked out of her by his own uncaring hands, and all that was really left between them was a bitter enmity mutually felt, and a refusal on his part to let go of something he considered his property.

On a mental shrug, she turned her attention to the dinner-trolley, intending to serve up the melon Guy had ordered as a first course, but his hand, coming tightly around her slender wrist, brought her attention sharply back to him. He was glaring at her, his dark brown eyes brooding and intent.

'I cannot pretend to know what was just going on behind that false smile of yours, Marnie, but I do warn you, most sincerely, to take care.'

The warning shivered through her. She might pride herself on being no one's fool, but neither was Guy. 'All I want to do is eat my dinner,' she said. 'You did promise me dinner and a bed, didn't you? So let me eat, then find the bed.'

'My bed,' he agreed with grim satisfaction, letting go of her wrist and sitting back in his chair, relaxing because he believed she'd walked herself right into that trap when really it was she doing the trapping.

'My own bed,' she corrected, placing large spoonfuls of the beautifully prepared melon into two dishes before passing one to him. 'I'll be sleeping alone tonight and every night until we are married again,' she flatly informed him.

'You'll sleep where I tell you to sleep, when I let you sleep,' he countered, just as flatly.

Marnie turned her attention to the melon, taking a small square into her mouth and murmuring at the sweetly delicious taste. 'This is very good,' she announced. 'Try it. It has something added to it that gives it a fantastic tangy flavour.'

He ignored her. 'We have a bargain, Marnie,' he reminded her. 'I dig your brother out of his mess and you——'

'Which reminds me,' she cut in on him. 'I must give Jamie a ring and let him know he can stop worrying. I'd forgotten all about him, poor thing.'

'There is no need for you to speak to Jamie,' Guy interrupted her drifting thoughts, 'because I have already done so.'

'Oh.' She glanced ruefully at him. 'I hope you didn't rip him into shreds—he's frightened enough of you as it is.'

'It seems a pity that his sister does not possess the same healthy instinct,' he muttered.

'If you'd wanted a simpering idiot for a wife, Guy,' she mocked, 'then you would not have looked twice at me.'

'True.' He smiled, relaxing enough at last to begin enjoying his melon. 'It has always been a big regret of mine that I did not take my own advice on that first day we met, and just turn tail and run in the other direction before I did take that—fatal second look.'

His eyes gleamed at her and Marnie grimaced, knowing exactly what he meant. Until he had met her, Guy had been used to women simpering all over him. He had been used to them sending out promises to him with their eyes, using every sexual lure in the book to attract his attention. He could handle all that by either responding or ignoring it depending on his mood. Marnie, by contrast, had never gone out of her way to attract him—and if anything had done everything she could to freeze him out. Guy had done all the running, all the careful luring—until the days and weeks of patient but fruitless persuasion eventually turned him into a quick-tempered and very frustrated man while Marnie, though half out of her mind in love with him, had continued to hold herself aloof, pretending to even be a little amused by his attention.

The bream was all it promised to be, and they managed to finish their meal in a companionable manner, both deliberately keeping the conversation light after that. The new mood suited Marnie. Having planted the seed of doubt about their sleeping arrangements tonight, she was quite happy to let that seed take root before she tackled the problem again. She wasn't worried; she knew she could win this one. Guy was an honourable man in his own way, and it was to that honour she was going to plead.

So it was gone ten o'clock before they both sat back in their seats and away from their empty coffee-cups, and Marnie stretched into a tired yawn which announced that she was more than ready for bed. 'Can

I borrow one of your shirts to sleep in?' she asked, getting to her feet.

Guy rose more slowly, the relaxed mood they'd managed to maintain throughout the meal shot to death. 'You will need no shirt to keep you warm tonight, Marnie,' he informed her smoothly, 'for I will be right beside you to ensure you do not catch a chill.'

Marnie paused in her movement away from the dining-table and took her time turning back to face him with a look of grave contemplation. 'You know, Guy,' she said quietly, 'for all that has gone between us—and some of it I accept has not been particularly nice—I have never once doubted that you respected me deeply as a person.'

The remark took him completely by surprise, sending him erect in a way that said she'd activated his enormous banks of pride. 'Which I do,' he immediately confirmed.

'And before we were married the last time—and no matter how—passionately you desired me, you always managed to demonstrate that respect by drawing back before you became too—carried away.'

He nodded curtly. 'You are referring, no doubt, to the fact that I wished my bride to come to me innocent on our wedding night.'

'Quite,' she agreed, unexpectedly touched by the degree of reverence he'd placed in that statement. 'You do know, don't you, Guy,' she went on, holding his gaze steady with her own, 'that there has been no other man but you in my life?'

His eyes blazed with a pride and a triumph he could not contain. 'I accept that—totally.' His trust in her was unequivocal—another fact which unexpectedly warmed her. 'It—it has always humbled me, Marnie,' he murmured huskily, 'that you can be so pure of heart and body when I know the depth of the passion which runs in your veins. Are you afraid that I may hurt you?' he asked suddenly, completely misunderstanding the point she was trying to make. He came around the table to take her shoulders in a gentle reassuring grip. 'I am very aware of the length of time it has been since we made love with each other, Marnie. And I am hungry for you—quite desperate in fact to feel your body warm and responsive beneath my own again, but my loving will be as gentle as it was the first time I took you as my own. You have nothing to fear from me.'

'No—you've...'

Misunderstood, she had been about to say. But his mouth was drowning out the telling word before it reached her lips, and nothing, nothing in all her careful planning prepared her for the kind of kiss he offered her, though perhaps his words should have done as he began to kiss her with such exquisite sweetness that she felt herself being hurled back across five long years to that moment on their wedding night when Guy had taken her in his arms as his wife.

And Marnie, with that memory filling her mind, responded, her mouth clinging to his while she tried desperately to untangle the past from the present, tried to remember why she was here and who she was with and what he would do to her if she so much as lowered her defences an inch. But the kiss was special, tender, loving, offering promises she'd once yearned for with all her heart. And as he gently urged her closer to the hard-packed, powerful wall of his chest she let herself relax, let her arms creep hungrily around his neck, let her lips part and their tongues meet and the heady, hot tide of desire wash languidly over her.

'Marnie,' he whispered against her clinging mouth. 'Sweet—sweet heaven.'

Then he brought her tumbling back down to a horrified sense of what was actually happening as he bent to lift her into his arms.

'No——!' she cried, twisting away from him before he'd managed to do more than flex his muscles in readiness to lift her.

He staggered slightly at her sudden escape, and Marnie found herself standing, swaying dizzily barely a foot away from him, breathing hectically, her eyes dark and glowing with a crazy mixture of self-aimed fury and deep disturbing sensuality.

'What do you mean, no?' he demanded in husky-voiced bewilderment.

Marnie swallowed, having to fight for breath before she could answer. 'I w-won't be seduced into your bed, Guy,' she whispered.

'And why not?' he demanded arrogantly. 'It was a mutual seduction, Marnie. I was being beautifully seduced also.'

Her cheeks coloured then went pale because she knew he was telling the truth. She had lost all control of herself for a moment there, had been more than matching him kiss for hungry, seductive kiss.

'You're used to it. I'm not.'

He stiffened. 'What is that supposed to mean?' he demanded.

'It means,' she said, outwardly beginning to pull herself back together, although inside she was a quivering, shivering wreck, 'that I expect you to treat me with the respect you've just claimed you always had for me by allowing me to keep my body for my husband alone.'

Silence, as he stared at her with a slow dawning understanding that took the light of passion out of his eyes, to be replaced with a look of hard, cynical appreciation when he realised just how cleverly she had been manipulating him all evening. 'You truly are the most cruel and calculating bitch of my acquaintance,' he then said, quite casually.

Her chin came up, defiance masking the sudden twinge of remorse she experienced inside. 'I can't ever forgive you, Guy,' she told him flatly. 'And although I also can't deny that you—you can make me want you physically, I'll never let you touch my heart again.'

'When did you ever?' he drawled, and turned away from her, but not before she'd glimpsed the look of bitterness in his eyes. 'Go.' He waved a careless hand towards the sitting-room door. 'Go to your cold and lonely bed, Marnie,' he invited. 'Take your high-minded principles and your unforgiving heart with you, since they seem to be the kind of bed partners you prefer. But remember this,' he added as he turned back to face her grimly. 'We have made a bargain tonight. And I expect you to stick to your side of it as fully as I intend to stick to mine. The day we become man and wife again, Marnie,' he ordained, 'will also be the day you will accept me back into your bed, and I will expect both the principles and the unforgiving heart to step aside for me.'

'Then you expect too much,' she said, forcing herself to move towards the sitting-room door.

'And why do I?' he posed silkily. 'I always believed, Marnie, that one first had to care to hurt as badly as you profess to do.'

'I cared,' she said, spinning back to face him. 'Or why else did I marry you?'

His smile was both mocking and self-derisive. 'I thought we both knew the answer to that, my dear. Because I gave you no damned choice.'

CHAPTER FIVE

NO CHOICE. Well, of everything he'd said tonight, Guy had been most right about that. If she had been given any choice at all, she would never have let him talk her into marrying him.

Bullied, Marnie corrected, and smiled bleakly into the dark silence which shrouded her in her bed. From the first moment he had ever set eyes on her Guy had pursued, seduced and bullied her until eventually she had wilted under the strain of it all and finally let him marry her.

Sighing, she turned on to her side to gaze sleeplessly out on to the clear navy blue sky beyond her bedroom window.

The first time she'd seen Guy, she had fancifully believed herself to have stumbled across some noble throwback from the last century.

He reminded her of the wicked baron portrayed in so many hot romantic novels. Big, dark and dangerous, with just enough charm to make the cynicism etched into his handsome face bearable. And more than enough sex appeal to make her heart quiver with a fatal mixture of excitement and alarm.

Of course, she'd known exactly who Jamie worked for that day she had decided on the spur of the moment to make a flying visit to her brother, but she hadn't for one moment expected actually to meet the man himself. What she knew about Guy Frabosa had been learned from newspaper and magazine articles—most of them painting a picture of a man who lived and slept with his ego. But they also presented a man who spent most of his busy life jetting around the world keeping the family empire running smoothly, and so she had driven through the tall wrought-iron gates of Oaklands expecting to see nothing more than her oil-smeared brother in his element, working on one of the many high-performance cars in Guy Frabosa's collection which he helped maintain, then leave again, completely untouched by the personality of the man who paid her brother's wages.

Coming upon Oaklands itself, nestling in its own small private valley, had been an artist's delight. And as she'd driven down the gently rolling hillside into the basin of the valley itself and cut across a wide stretch of tarmac roadway towards the elegant cream-painted Georgian mansion house she could see in the distance, it had never occurred to her that she had just driven over Guy Frabosa's own personal racing track, or that it circumvented the whole estate, built by professionals for a professional to practise upon. Her concentration then had been too enthralled by the beauty of the gardens she had been passing through.

I could sit and paint this forever, she recalled thinking as she brought the car to a stop in the circular courtyard in front of the house and climbed out of her battered old Mini to absorb the wonderful air of peace and tranquillity around her. The air smelled fresh and country-clean, weighed down with the heady scent of roses—roses she had not known then were Roberto Frabosa's pride and joy.

It was the distinctive throaty roar of a powerful engine revving that had told her in which direction to go looking for her brother, and she had followed the sound around the side of the house and along a pretty winding path through a narrow wood until she found herself standing on the edge of a courtyard that must once have been the stable-yard, but now housed the workshops and garages for Guy's impresive collection of cars.

And it was there, while she stood beneath the shelter of a spreading chestnut tree, that she had experienced her first shock sighting of the man she had later married...

He was standing like a Michelangelo's David among a clutch of Lowrie figures as his team of mechanics clustered around him, towering over them as he talked, his dark head thrown up at an arrogant angle while his mouth, firm and shockingly sensual, was stretched into a grin which completely belied the arrogance.

They were talking engines, of course, but then Marnie could only appreciate the sheer artistry of the scene—he, Guy, thrown into strong stomach-churning contrast, in his crisp white shirt and immaculate dark trousers, to the murky cluster of oil-stained-overalled men gathered about him.

A king with his minions, she titled the scene, already capturing it in oils in her mind. He spoke quickly but smoothly, the rich timbre of his voice, attractively spiced with an accent, reaching out to her across the cobbled courtyard to keep her held breathless and still.

Her experience of the opposite sex then was poor to say the least; not finding the time to learn about them had been the main culprit for her ignorance because she'd never seemed to have enough of it to spare for the lighter side of living. But even she, wrapped in the protection of her complete innocence, could pick up danger signals when they were there.

'Marnie!' It was Jamie who saw her first. And she just had time to see Guy's dark head turn sharply, glimpse the sudden narrowing of his dark eyes, note the tensing stillness of his body, before she dragged her wide eyes away from him and forced them to rest on her brother.

Jamie came over to her, so pleased to see her that he was grinning from ear to ear. 'What are you doing here?' he demanded in surprise.

She told him, trying desperately not to allow her attention to wander over to where she knew Guy was watching them with that same silent stillness he hadn't even tried to snap out of since their eyes clashed.

'But this is great!' her brother exclaimed. 'Can you stay long enough to have lunch with me? There's a pub just down the road from here that puts on a great ploughman's; we could——'

'Introduce me, Jamie.'

Just like that, she recalled. Introduce me. Make me known. I want. Give me. Mine. It had all been there in that one huskily voiced demand.

Not that her brother noticed any of that as he happily complied, moving a step away from her to leave her feeling oddly exposed and very vulnerable to that hot dark stare. 'This is my sister, Marnie,'

Jamie announced. 'Marnie, meet my employer, Mr Frabosa.'

'Guy,' corrected the man himself, letting the true pronunciation of his name slide sensually off his tongue.

He lifted a long, tanned, beautifully constructed hand to her in invitation for her to take it. She did so nervously, trembling a little, a bit bewildered by what was happening to her churning insides, and shaken even more off balance when instead of the polite handshake she had been expecting he lifted her hand to his lips, his eyes refusing to break contact with the dense blueness of hers.

It had taken him just that long to make her fall head over heels in love with him—not that she'd understood what it was then. Because she was unawakened to her own sexuality and quite content to stay that way, that sudden overpowering burst of emotion had frightened her then—it still did now. But then she had been in no way equipped to deal with it, and the fact that he was making no effort to hide how powerfully she attracted him had the adverse effect of sending her scuttling off in the other direction. She snatched her hand away and took a jerky but very necessary step back from him, and he smiled at her in a way that mocked her small rejection.

He invited her to take tea in his home. She refused, reminding him coolly that it was her brother she had come here to see. When Guy then blandly informed her that Jamie would not be free from his duties until the evening and repeated the invitation while she waited for her brother to finish his work, she glanced ruefully at her brother, who was looking bemused at

Guy's announcement, and still refused to allow him to act host in her brother's absence, inventing a fictitious date waiting for her in London which brought Jamie's gaze swinging around to her in open-mouthed amazement, since he was well aware of her lack of interest in the kind of date she was implying. 'I can only stay five minutes at most,' she added hurriedly, wishing she had not given in to the sudden urge to come and see her brother.

Guy stared at her, bringing a guilty flush to her cheeks because the mockery in his gaze said he knew she was lying, and with a bow and a smile that did nothing to ease her anxious desire to get away from him he excused himself and strode off towards the front of the house while Jamie stared after him in frowning confusion.

'I don't understand any of that,' he gasped. 'Guy isn't usually so...'

'Five minutes, Western!' The curt warning had come from the disappearing figure of Guy Frabosa as he rounded the corner of the house.

'I don't understand that, either!' Jamie exclaimed. 'Why were you so cool with him, Marnie?' he demanded, deciding that the blame for it all had to belong to her. 'I thought it was very nice of him to welcome you like that—and you turn all icy on him—you've offended him now!'

'I came to see you, Jamie,' she reminded her brother coolly. 'Not to take tea with a man who is a complete stranger to me.'

He shrugged, still baffled by the whole odd encounter, and walked her back around the house to her car, chatting lightly, but she could tell he was jumpy, eager to get back to work before Guy decided to come down on him a second time. And she was more than ready to get away before his boss disturbed her level senses a second time. Jamie saw her seated behind the wheel of her Mini, quizzing her on how it was running, and smiling when she assured him the little car gave her no trouble at all, her eyes skipping nervously along the rows of windows in the house, somehow knowing that Guy Frabosa was observing her departure from the shadows somewhere inside.

She turned the key in the ignition, now quite desperate to get away.

Nothing happened. She tried again. Nothing.

After several tries, her brother muttered something derogatory about stupid women flooding the engine, and ordered her out so he could get in instead. He messed, he fiddled, then climbed out and lifted the bonnet, disappearing beneath it with all the concentration of a born mechanic while Marnie stood, knowing, without knowing how she knew, that her car had not let her down without help from somewhere.

She watched Guy stroll out of the front door with a fatalistic acceptance that must have shown on her face, because he sent her a lazy mocking look as he went to join her brother.

A small smile touched her lips as she lay now in her bed with only the moon as witness. It was months later before Guy had actually admitted to doctoring her car.

'I was not prepared to let you go,' he had told her with all the lazy arrogance of his nature.

'Did Jamie know it was your doing?' she'd demanded.

'Since it took him five hours to find the fault, I would have to presume that, on finding it, he must have guessed,' Guy had answered blandly. 'He is too good a mechanic not to have realised quite early on that the car had been tampered with. His problem was discovering just what it was I had done to it.'

'Sometimes, Guy, I hate your arrogance.'

'And sometimes, *cara*, you literally drown in it,' he'd growled, pulling her into his arms to prove his point. She had had no control whatsoever of the passion he could arouse in her. And even in the very early days of their relationship, when he was very aware of her inexperience, he had been able to turn her blood to fire with an ease that had both shocked and frightened her.

A fear that had kept her fighting him right through the turbulent weeks which had followed as Guy, true to the stubborn, selfish character he was, set himself out to take what he wanted.

And take he eventually had. Ruthlessly, passionately, unassailingly and with scant regard to whether or not it was what she wanted. Or maybe he did regard it but chose to dismiss it, she allowed. Because even Guy, thick-skinned as he was, had to know that although he had forced her to surrender physically to him he had never really managed to beat down her mental reserves towards him.

Sighing wearily, Marnie gave up trying to stop the memories from coming, and climbed out of bed to go and stand by the moonlit window.

Marriage to Guy had been no less fraught than their turbulent courtship. He'd decided on marriage, he'd informed her then, because he just could not bring himself to take her innocence without the legal right to do so. And she had been so damned weakened by his sensual assaults on her that she'd foolishly agreed.

So married they were, and he took her off to his native Italy where, in a secluded villa overlooking his own private piece of the Med, he taught her all there was to learn about the physical side of love. And he possessed her to such a devastating degree that he only had to look at her to make her want him. True to his nature, he had no inhibitions about the forms their lovemaking could take, and taught her to cast off any she might have wanted to hold on to. Her body became an instrument tuned like one of his precious cars to his own personal specification, and for six dizzy, passionate months they drifted through life in a haze of mutual engrossment where the only cloud cluttering their sensual haven was a distinct absence of any sincere words of love.

Guy seemed only to require the delight of her young and responsive body, while she—well, she just accepted what crumbs of himself he threw at her and kept a vital part of herself hidden away from him in readiness for the time when the novelty would die and he would begin looking about him for pastures new.

And why did she think it would come to that? Because she had seen the way he was around other women. Guy was a born egotist, forever needing to feed that ego through the constant adoration of any woman prepared to offer it to him.

She suspected that he didn't really see her as a living, breathing person with thoughts and feelings of her own but more like a new possession he liked to show off to his friends—like a mascot, kept for his own amusement. It never occurred to him that she wouldn't like his friends, that the constant vying for the centre of attention by both sexes and the suggestive remarks that were thrown about so freely actually shocked and embarrassed her.

Shy by nature, she was always rather quiet and withdrawn in company, and they felt no qualms about teasing her about her quietness, making her feel more uncomfortable in their company, showing her in their cruel, deriding way that she was not and never would be one of them.

On top of that, she had to grin and bear the sight of Guy enjoying the over-amorous advances of one or other of the many women who threw themselves at him. He was that kind of man: handsome, worldly, and full of a charisma that had been earned by the dangerous way he'd achieved his fame. Women adored him, and he took their adoration entirely as his due, and wasn't past encouraging it when the mood took him.

It was witnessing one of the more—obvious displays of adoration one night that decided Marnie that she'd had enough.

The party was being held by one of Guy's old racing cronies, in a big London town-house with several reception-rooms packed to bursting with people enjoying themselves in their brittle, sophisticated way. She had learned early on that there were no holds barred at these functions. Drink yourself silly if you wanted to, make passes at anyone you fancy—which did not count her out just because she was the great Guy Frabosa's wife! And it was even acceptable for some couples to disappear for a significant length of time during the evening, and not always with the person they'd arrived with! It forced her to wonder about the times she couldn't find Guy in the crush these parties always were; to wonder if he too was not averse to sneaking off for a quick tumble with some willing creature.

But that particular night, the crunch came for Marnie when it happened to be Anthea Cole who decided to drape herself around him from the moment they arrived, and not let go since. Anthea was the woman Marnie had usurped from Guy's bed. And to see her of all people hanging all over him, knowing that the other woman was as knowledgeable about Guy's lovemaking as she was herself, just about blew her usual cool as a hard, hot, ugly sting of jealousy ripped through her. Then, to top it all, seeing Guy busy with Anthea, Derek Fowler had the gall to chance his arm with Marnie! She slapped him down, coldly and precisely, leaving him in absolutely no doubt what she thought of him, then walked out of the party, leaving Guy to do as he pleased.

He was furious, of course. When he arrived back at the apartment he came storming into their bedroom where she was emerging from the adjoining bathroom after a long, hot, angry shower, rubbing at her wet hair with a towel.

'What the hell is the matter with you?' he snapped, slamming the door shut so hard that she winced.

'What the bloody hell were you trying to prove, walking out on me in front of my friends?'

'You call them friends?' she scoffed. 'I call them a bunch of ravenous wolves, existing for only one thing in life—sex!' she said in disgust. 'Wherever and however they can get it. And if they are your friends, then for God's sake don't count me as one of them; I don't think I could live with the taint of it!' She spun away from him, the towel rubbing furiously at her long wet hair.

'Someone has offended you,' he said, coming down from his own anger because he thought he could soothe away hers now he knew the reason for it.

'You could say that,' she snapped. '*You've* offended me. You offend me every time you take me to parties like that one we went to tonight.' She turned to view the look of surprise written on his hard, handsome face. 'You then consolidate the offence by just dropping me to go in search of your own pleasures in another woman's arms while expecting me to stand meekly by and await your wonderful return!'

'Anthea,' he said. 'You're angry because you're jealous of Anthea!'

He sounded so damned self-satisfied that Marnie actually did bare her nails and her teeth as she shouted, 'Anthea? What the hell is Anthea except for one in a long long line of Antheas who've been led to believe that you're open to anything they want to offer you? Well, not this woman any more!' Angrily, she threw the towel aside and walked threateningly towards him. 'Because this woman has more self-respect than to sleep with an ageing old stallion who sees his main function in life as putting himself out for stud!'

Oh, she shouldn't have said it. And even now, all these years later, she could still feel the clutch of remorse she'd felt then as she watched his face go pale, and his body jerk as if in reaction to a vicious blow.

And vicious it had been, because she'd known how sensitive Guy was to the difference in their ages. It was perhaps his one and only Achilles' heel, and she'd cruelly pierced it dead in the centre.

Of course, he went all cold and haughty on her. It was perhaps either that or seduce her senseless. She'd deserved both. But it was the haughtiness she got, and with such devastating impact that she could even find it in her to admire him for it now. Though not then—not then when he said coldly, 'Then, of course, you must sleep alone, my dear Marnie. While I, poor ageing stud that I am, will go out and find a less discerning creature to share my humble bed.'

Which he had, she recalled bitterly now. He left the apartment and did not come back for three days—by which time she had gone from remorse to resentment and from there to an angry defiance which had her accepting a commission which took her off to Manchester for a week.

She arrived back tired, miserable and so riddled with guilt for those terrible words she had thrown at him that she was quite prepared to go down on her knees and beg so long as he forgave her for them. It was late, and Guy was already in bed when she let herself quietly into their bedroom. She wasn't sure if he was awake, but she sensed that he was as she crossed to the bathroom and quickly showered before going and climbing into the bed beside him.

He didn't say a word, not a single word, but the way he reached for her was a message in itself, and they made love with a kind of wild desperation that shook them both. But if she had been secretly hoping he would reassure her about those other women then she was disappointed, and a new restraint entered their relationship, the strain that last row had placed between them always hovering in the tense air around them.

Nothing was really the same after that. They went to no more parties. That complaint at least had seemed to get through to him. But Guy treated her with a new kind of respect which verged on indifference, while she threw herself into her work, accepting commissions wherever they were offered which took her away from London for long days on end. And Guy had his own commitments to fulfil, flying off to all corners of the world, so they became more like strangers than husband and wife, meeting briefly in the darkness of their bedroom to slake a hunger that was all the more wretched because it was all they seemed to have.

The strain of it all became too much for Marnie, and a depression began to set in. She came back home after spending a miserable week in Kent to find the apartment empty because Guy was away somewhere in the wilds of Yorkshire. He was away a week, and by the time he came back she was feeling so low that he took one hard look at her pale, unhappy face and gathered her into his arms.

She thought he was after sex, and retaliated accordingly by pushing him angrily away. So he did his usual, and bit out some deriding words at her about what a mess she looked and how he was going out to find someone who knew how to keep her man. He didn't return that night. When he did, he looked as though he had just rolled out of someone's bed to come straight home.

They had another row—one which ended up with him bundling her into his car and taking her to Oaklands. Where he left her—to decide, he said, which was more important to her: her marriage or her work.

It was the first time he had challenged the amount of time she devoted to her work. And she read it clearly for what it was: an ultimatum. He wanted total devotion or nothing, and for the next week she seethed bitterly over the choice, wishing she could just up and leave him and knowing wretchedly that she could not. She loved him too much.

Then something happened to make the decision for her. And suddenly she was in a fever of excitement, racing back to London to see Guy.

She arrived at the apartment in time for dinner, but Guy wasn't there and Mrs Dukes, the housekeeper, said she had hardly seen him since Marnie went away. Casting aside the small sting of alarm she experienced, she set about ringing around in an effort to find him. Calling her brother was just a spur-of-the-moment idea. Guy had recently set Jamie up in his own small garage just outside London, and she knew he liked to call in and show an interest in whatever car Jamie was working on at the time.

'Have you tried Derek Fowler's house?' he suggested. 'There's some kind of big party going on there tonight, so I heard. Perhaps Guy has gone there.

You should keep a tighter rein on that man of yours, Marnie,' he then went on to admonish. 'Guy is too hot a property for you to let run around London as freely as he does. Women just can't keep their hands off him.'

But they will learn, she thought grimly as she set out for the party. From now on, all of them will learn that Guy Frabosa is well and truly taken!

She arrived at Derek Fowler's home to find the party in full swing. She and Derek Fowler had become cold antagonists since she'd slapped him down, so stepping over the threshold into his house took a certain amount of courage. But she was desperate to see Guy, and that was all that was in her mind as she squeezed a way through the crush of people to go in search of him, having no idea just what she was walking into.

It took just ten minutes to find out.

She found Derek Fowler first, flirting lazily with a slinky model type wearing a red silk dress and nothing else, by the look of it.

'Is Guy here?' she asked him coolly.

He turned slightly bloodshot eyes on her, and the lazy smile he had been wearing changed into a taunting leer. 'Well, well, well,' he drawled. 'If it isn't the child bride herself.'

'Is he here?' she repeated coldly, refusing to rise to the bait. Guy hated it when his friends referred to her in that way. He was sensitive enough about their age-difference without having 'cradle-snatcher' thrown at him.

'Upstairs, I think,' he informed her carelessly. 'Second door on the right, sleeping off the old plonko the last time I saw him . . .' Something else caught his attention then, sending his gaze narrowing over to the stairs, which were just visible through the crush of people spilling out into the hallway. When he looked back at Marnie there was a new vindictive light in his narrowed eyes. 'Why don't you go and wake the prince with a kiss?' he suggested silkily. 'You never know, Marnie, you might even get a nice surprise.'

Not understanding the taunt—and not even trying to—she turned away, struggling back through the crowds towards the hallway and from there up the stairs, sighing with relief at the respite from the noise and the crush of bodies on the floor below.

It was dark inside the room Derek had directed her to. She stepped inside and fumbled blindly for the light switch. 'Guy?' she called out softly. 'Guy, are you awake?'

Light flooded the room, and at the same cataclysmic moment that she heard the muffled murmur of her name Marnie stood frozen by the horror of what she was being forced to recognise as Guy's beautiful body lying naked in a tumble of white bedding, with the lovely Anthea coiled intimately around him—as naked as he.

CHAPTER SIX

'CAN'T you sleep?' a quiet voice enquired behind her. Marnie started violently, spinning around too quickly to mask the pain her memories had laid naked on her face. Guy saw the look, knew its source, and his own expression closed in grim response to it.

He was leaning against the open doorway, dark hair ruffled by restless fingers as if he too had been having a struggle with sleep. And for once he looked his age, harsh lines pulling at his lean features, scoring deep grooves down the sides of his nose and the taut turned-down corners of his mouth.

Older, but still the same potently sexual man who drew the opposite sex to him like bees to honey, she acknowledged bleakly as her eyes made a swift sweep of his tightly muscled body covered only by the short black robe before looking quickly away. He could still stir her senses just by being in the same room, and she hated herself for it—hated herself.

'My shirt looks better on you than it does on me,' he murmured huskily. 'But then, they always did.'

Her body began to tingle in instant response to the lazy way he ran his eyes over the fine silk shirt she had taken from his room before retiring, sending her arms wrapping around her body as the tingle centred itself in the very tips of her sensitive nipples.

'What do you want, Guy?' she demanded stiffly.

'You,' he answered without hesitation. 'But since that is nothing new to either of us,' he added drily, 'and since we both seem unable to sleep tonight, I wondered if you would like to share a pot of tea with me?'

'Tea?' Sheer surprise diverted her away from the provocation in the earlier remark. 'Since when have you been drinking tea?'

Guy had always shown a scathing contempt for the English love of the beverage. He liked coffee, strong and black and sugarless.

'Actually——' an oddly sheepish smile took the harshness out of his features '—I was going to treat myself to a brandy. The suggestion of tea was an afterthought—offered as an incentive for you to join me. Will you?'

Slowly, tentatively almost, his hand came out in front of him. Marnie stared unblinkingly at it for a moment. A long, strong, capable hand, a hand she knew so intimately that it was like an extension of her own self. A hand which seemed to be offering more than just an invitation to join him.

Her glance flicked warily to his face, but found nothing to mistrust written there, just a wry twist of a smile that said he was quite ready for her usual rebuttal.

'Well...?' he murmured softly.

'Yes,' she heard herself say. 'Yes, I'd like that.' Why, she had no idea, except maybe she found suddenly that she didn't want to be alone, and even Guy's company was better than the kind of cold company her black thoughts had been to her.

Easing himself away from the door as she drew near, he let her brush by him before falling into step behind her. The door to his own bedroom stood open, the soft glow from his bedside lamp illuminating the stacks of papers littered about his untidy bed telling their own story.

'You know me, Marnie,' he murmured. 'I need little sleep.'

No, four hours a night was just about his limit, she recalled. As to the rest of the hours of darkness—well, Guy had had his own method of amusing himself, a method that was best not dwelt upon right now.

She curled herself up in the corner of the sofa while he prepared the tea. He wasn't such a chauvinist that he'd ever minded taking on such a menial task. In fact, Marnie could recall several times when he had wandered into her studio in their London apartment with a tea-tray in his hands.

'Drink it,' he had used to command; peer over her shoulder at whatever she was working on, give no opinion whatsoever, brush a light kiss across the exposed nape of her neck, then walk out again, whistling quietly to himself.

They'd been married for several months before it had dawned on her that he only used the tea as an excuse to enter what was essentially her domain. If she turned and smiled at him he used to grin and pull her into his arms for a good long kiss before walking out again. If she ignored him, she used to receive that peck on the neck before he wandered out, whistling. But he never tried to break her concentration.

'Why?' she asked him once.

'You have two great passions in your life, Marnie,' he said. 'One is your work and the other is me. When you are working, your art takes precedence. I am man enough to accept second place on those occasions so long as, once your work is done, I then fill your world.'

It was a shame he had not applied the same philosophy to himself.

'Here.' He offered her a cup and saucer.

'Thank you.' She took it from him, then watched as he took his brandy glass and threw himself down in the chair opposite her, his weariness showing in the long sigh he gave as he stretched himself out, long tanned legs with their liberal covering of crisp dark hair extending beyond the black silk covering of his brief robe.

Marnie swallowed drily, lowering her eyes to the steaming brew in her cup. Looking at him hurt. It always had, even when they'd been supposedly happy. He was that kind of man, painfully, heartbreakingly beautiful.

'How is your father?' she enquired, as a direct snub to the kind of thinking she had been about to indulge in.

'Resigned to using a walking stick, at last.' Guy grimaced. Roberto, like his son, had his fair share of pride. When a slight stroke had left a stiffness down one side of his body, he had not taken kindly to the idea of using a stick to get about. 'He has a different stick for all occasions now,' he added drily. 'Your doing, I suspect.' There was a half-question in his mocking gaze.

Marnie smiled. 'I just happened to mention to him—in passing, you know—how interesting a man of his good looks and charm could look sporting a walking stick.'

'You mean you pandered to his ego.'

'The Italian in him,' she corrected. 'Goodness, but you Latin types place so much importance on your outward appearance,' she complained. 'I don't think there is a race of people more egotistical, arrogant, proud——'

'It was all of those things which attracted you to me once,' Guy mildly pointed out.

She ignored the remark. 'I thought,' she went on consideringly instead, 'that since I have to be in Berkshire myself next week I might call in to see him on my way. I could perhaps beg dinner and a bed for the night, then I can spend the whole evening flattering him a little before I need to be on my way.'

'We shall certainly be going to Oaklands,' Guy murmured slowly, watching her through hooded eyes. 'But, as to anything you have planned in Berkshire, I am afraid you will have to cancel it.'

Marnie uncurled her legs from beneath her, alarm skittering along her spine. 'What do you mean?' she demanded sharply.

Guy yawned lazily. 'Exactly what you think I meant,' he said, getting up to pour himself another drink. 'As from tonight, you became my property again—which means you'll be taking no more commissions which take you away from home.'

'I won't give up my work for you, Guy!' she stated sharply.

'You will do exactly as I say,' he informed her, quite casually, as though the subject did not warrant him raising his voice to it. 'Accept, Marnie—just as my father has had to accept his walking stick—that you are mine again, and in so being your commitments to me will override any others you may have already made.'

'Not my work.' She shook her head adamantly. 'I will not give up my work and—dammit, Guy, but you can't make me!'

'I can,' he assured her, 'and I intend to.'

The sardonic raising of his brows brought her climbing furiously to her feet. 'But y-you let me continue working the last time we were together!' she choked. 'I——'

'Just one of the mistakes I made in our marriage,' he declared. 'One which will be corrected this time around.'

Struggling to maintain a grasp on her sanity, Marnie tried to be reasonable. In all honesty, she had not expected this. Of all the other horrors she had forced herself to think about concerning the situation, this was one she had not even so much as considered!

'But—my work is my life!' she cried. 'You know it is! You can't just——'

'I can do whatever I please,' he cut in with infuriating calm. 'One of the most fundamental errors I made when dealing with you before, Marnie, was——'

'Sleeping around!' she snapped out bitterly.

His curt nod was an acknowledgment of a direct hit, but barely rattled his composure. 'Was allowing you,' he went on regardless of her outburst, 'too much of your own way. I let you roam about the countryside like a gypsy with hardly a complaint. I let you choose which friends I could keep and which I had to discard. I...'

'You didn't discard Anthea, I made painful note!'

'I let you, Marnie,' he continued grimly, 'run my life to such an extent that I began to lose my own identity!'

'*You* lost *your* identity?' she scoffed out scornfully. 'What do you think our marriage did for me? I became Guy Frabosa's woman! The silly child-bride who was as naïve as she was blind!'

'But that is just the point,' Guy put in silkily. 'You are no longer a child, Marnie. Remember that, because I don't intend to treat you as one. This time you will be a proper wife to me—a full-time wife! The kind of wife every man who is honest with himself wants in a marriage, which is the old-fashioned, home-loving, child-bearing kind!'

Her face drained of colour, the uncaring arrogance of his words hurting her in a way Guy would never know. 'God, how I hate you!' she whispered, teeth clenched and chattering in the bloodless tension in her face.

'And what a passionate hatred it is,' he derided. 'For if I touched you now, Marnie, while you *hate* so spectacularly, you would go up in flames, and you know it!' With a condemning flick of his black gaze he glanced down her quivering body, missing nothing, not the hectic heave of her breasts or the damning evidence of her nipples pushing hard and tight against the fine white silk covering of his shirt. 'Your body yearns for mine,' he accused condemningly. 'That is why you fight so hard against your own desires, Marnie: because you want me. Want me so badly that it was a relief to you when your brother gave you the opportunity to place yourself at my mercy!'

'That's a lie!' she rasped. 'I despise the very thought of you so much as touching me!'

'Is that so?' he murmured silkily, lifting his hand towards her in a way that had her shrinking shakily back from him.

'No decent woman would ever want you, Guy,' she threw at him contemptuously. 'Not one who has seen with her own eyes how freely you put yourself about!'

'You only saw what you think you saw!' he snapped, angry suddenly because the argument had taken a turn he had much rather it hadn't. 'But that period in our lives is no longer up for discussion,' he then stated grimly. 'I have tried too many times to make you listen while I explained it all to you; now I find I no longer want to. What has gone before today, Marnie, is now dead and gone, and must now be forgotten, because what follows in its wake will begin with a new set of rules which will leave no room for further dissension, on either side.'

Dead, gone, forgotten. Those three words echoed hollowly in her mind, bringing her swooping down from anger into weariness far more successfully than any attempt at subjugation on Guy's part.

'Let me continue working,' she requested. If he would just concede this one point to her, then perhaps, she hoped, she could manage to put the rest aside as he wanted her to do. 'The only thing I'll ask of you, Guy!' she pleaded when she saw the uncompromising set of his jaw. 'The rest I—promise to abide by, so long as I can at least have my work!'

'No compromises this time. I'm sorry.' He sounded it too, his tone rough but firm. 'But your work got in the way of us ever having a chance of making a success of our marriage the first time around. This time it has to be different.'

'And your other women?' she demanded. 'Do they stop also?'

'Do you want them to?' he enquired smoothly.

God. She closed her eyes, swallowing on the bank of bitterness lying like acid in her throat. 'Do what you want,' she sighed, turning towards the door. 'I find I don't give a damn!'

'Then why all this fuss?' he demanded. 'For someone who professes not to care at all, Marnie, you are giving a remarkable show of caring—perhaps too much?'

There was enough truth in that final taunt to sting her into spinning back to face him. 'I will always despise you for forcing me into accepting you back like this! Is that what you want?' she asked. 'A woman—a wife who will resent every moment she has to spend in your arms? Is the price *you're* going to pay for having me back in your life really worth the satisfaction you think you'll feel at managing it?'

'I know it will be,' he said, taking the single stride which brought his body hard up against her own. She took a jerky step back, and found her back pressed hard against the solid wood of the door.

'Let go of me,' she muttered, trying to push his hands away. 'Your touch makes my skin crawl!'

Guy smiled. 'Crawl with what, I wonder?' he murmured, placing his hands on her waist and crushing the fine silk fabric of his shirt against her naked flesh.

She began to tremble, tremble so badly that she could barely breathe. 'No,' she groaned as he began to lower his mouth to hers.

'No?' he taunted. 'Are you very sure of that?'

His mouth landed, splitting her sanity into a million atoms of pure sensation. He began slowly drawing the silk up her body, drawing her deeper and deeper into the kiss as he slowly—agonisingly almost—exposed the bottom half of her body then pressed the thrusting heat of his own against her. Her senses responded instantly, making her squirm in an effort to combat the flood of sensual delight that ran through her.

She felt drenched in her own desire; her mouth opened, parting to allow him to deepen the kiss. His hands reached the undercurve of her breasts, the silk bunched up beneath them, and on a smooth sensual movement he slid his fingers beneath to cup and lift her before knowingly brushing his thumbs across the waiting points of her nipples.

She moaned, moving instinctively against him, her hands dragging tensely up the sides of his lean body to clutch at the bunched muscles of his shoulder-blades. 'Stop it,' she gasped.

He ignored her. Her fingers clenched, then gripped hard, digging into the taut flesh beneath them as she fought the rage of feeling she was suffering inside. 'Why don't you just stop trying to fight me, Marnie?' Guy murmured seductively. 'You know you want to.'

'No——'

'Yes!' he insisted, and parted her lips with the sensual force of his own. It was a kiss like no other. Hungry, passionate, charged with an angry urgency that sent her senses spinning out of control. Hazily, she tried to stop herself responding. But it was too late; their tongues met in a wild tangling that set them both breathing harshly.

His hands moved, but before she had a chance to groan out in protest at losing their electric caress to her breasts they were sliding sensually down her body to cup possessively at her buttocks, and it was only as he thrust his lower body towards her that she realised he had untied his robe, and she stopped breathing altogether as he pushed the throbbing fullness of his manhood between her trembling thighs.

'God in heaven,' he breathed, dragging his mouth from hers so he could bury it in her throat.

Her face was pushed against the thick mat of crisp dark hair on his chest. She tried to pull herself together, sucking in deep gulps of air, but the thundering sound of his heartbeat against her parted mouth seemed to overwhelm everything. They were almost one. Their bodies melded so closely together that she felt drunk and dizzy with the pleasure of it. His fingers were tense and restless, kneading her tender flesh while her own had somehow found their way over his shoulders and were clinging to the muscled tautness of his neck.

He moved against her, just once, shuddered violently and stopped, his breathing so harsh that she realised just how close he was to losing complete control.

'Guy,' she whispered desperately, not really sure what she was pleading for.

'Give me back my promise, Marnie,' he pleaded huskily against her throat. 'I need to be inside you.'

Oh, God. She closed her eyes. This should not be happening. She should not be allowing this to happen! It was lust, she told herself madly. Sheer uncontrollable lust. The last time she had seen him this aroused, it had been in the arms of another woman.

'No——!' From somewhere she found the strength to push him away, sending him staggering backwards in surprise while she turned, trembling badly, to press her face into the door.

'Why not?' he rasped, his voice so raw she barely recognised it. 'You want me! You can no longer go on pretending you do not!'

'And for that I hate myself,' she confessed wretchedly. She spun round, eyes bright with pain and unshed tears. 'Can you even begin to know what it feels like to want a man you've seen with your own eyes beneath the naked body of another woman?'

Guy blanched, his hand coming up between them in abject appeal. 'No! Marnie, it——'

But she reeled away from him, her arms once more hugging herself protectively. 'No,' she choked, cutting him off before he could even begin the explanation she heard hovering on his tongue. 'Nothing—nothing can ever dismiss that vision from my mind, Guy. Nothing, do you understand?'

On a choking sob, she turned and fled from the room, taking that final bitter vision with her.

She could still replay, with vivid accuracy, that dreadful night she had found him in bed with Anthea.

He had not been long behind her in returning to their apartment, but finding her locked behind her studio door and refusing to answer his plea for her to open the door had driven him to kicking it down.

'Will you let me explain?' he had rasped, coming swaying to a halt as the solid wood door with its freshly splintered lock landed with a resounding crash against the wall behind it. 'It was not what you think!'

It was probably the only time she had ever seen him looking anything but immaculate. His clothes, hastily pulled on, hung about him. Shirt half fastened, trousers creased and beltless. Wherever his jacket had been, it had not been on his back. Face white and drawn, eyes wild, and his hair, that head of silky black hair, a crumpled mess—made that way by Anthea's fingers.

The memory of all of that still had the ability to crush her inside. A living nightmare four years on.

Her refusal to so much as look at him, never mind listen to him, had him dragging her against his violently shaking frame. 'Marnie,' he'd pleaded hoarsely. 'You have to listen to me!'

The stench of whisky had been strong, mingling with a cloying perfume that made her gag, his touch so repulsive to her that she had had to wrench herself free and run into the bathroom, where she was violently sick while Guy had stood, leaning heavily against the door-frame, watching her suffer with a look of hell in his eyes.

'I was drunk,' he'd said. 'I had been drinking steadily all day. I arrived at the party already slewed out of my mind. Derek took one look at me and pushed me up the stairs and into that room where he stripped me off and put me to bed. I never knew another thing until Anthea . . .'

She had turned on him then, her eyes touched with a kind of madness. The sickness had left her weak and shaky, but the bitterness and pain had been making the adrenalin pump hotly through her blood, and she had launched herself at him, her hand making violent contact with his face, her fingers, unknowingly set into claws, scoring into the taut flesh of his cheek.

He hadn't even flinched. He had just stood there staring at her, grim, white-faced and with tortured eyes, but passive.

She remembered standing there for a wild unaccountable moment watching the blood begin to trickle down his cheek, following its progress with a kind of dazed fascination, not really aware that she had actually inflicted the wound on him.

'I hate you,' she'd whispered then, in a voice so devoid of emotion that he had shuddered. 'You don't know what you've done to me, and I shall never forgive you—never.'

She had turned away, meaning to leave right there and then. But Guy had made the mistake of touching her, begging her again to just listen to him, and she had turned on him again, hitting out at him with her fist, her feet, showering blows on his body while once again he stood rock-solid-still and let her do her worst until, weak with exhaustion, she had collapsed against him, to sob brokenly into his gaping shirt.

Without a single word he had just picked her up in his arms and carried her through to their bedroom, where he'd laid her down and covered her with the duvet before turning and walking out of the room. Leaving her alone to weep.

She had been alone ever since.

CHAPTER SEVEN

'LOOK.' The grim tension simmering between them had not eased in the slightest over the last two miserable days, and Guy was at last sounding utterly fed up as he drove them from the airport into London. 'I am not prepared to argue about it any more! We are going directly to my apartment and that's where you will sleep tonight!'

Marnie's mouth was set in a petulant line, Guy's own expression not much better. The row about where she would sleep tonight had been going on since they'd boarded his private jet in Edinburgh. She was tired, irritable and depressed—the worst of those three things being the tiredness, since she had barely slept a wink during the two nights they had spent in Edinburgh. If she hadn't been lying there tossing and turning restlessly while she battled with her black memories, she had been lying there battling against the damned traitorous way her body wanted to remember how good Guy could make it feel if she would only give in and let him.

'I'm not intending running away, for God's sake,' she sighed wearily.

'No? Well, I am not prepared to trust your word on that. So stop nagging!'

'I only want to get a decent night's sleep in my own bed before I have to face your father tomorrow! God knows,' she complained, eyeing her sadly creased and unhappy dress with distaste, 'I must look a wreck! All I want now is a shower, a change of clothes and my own bed for one last night! I couldn't care less about running away, Guy! I don't think I have the energy left in me to try!' she added drily.

'You had the option to buy fresh clothes in Edinburgh. It was through your own stubbornness that you look a wreck. The rest you can get at the apartment,' he dismissed.

'But I could see to my packing tonight rather than having to do it tomorrow,' she attempted a bit of cajolery.

'No.'

She glared at him. 'Did you bully the girls when you were a little boy, too?' she threw at him tightly.

'I was known for my charm as a child, actually,' he answered with the first hint of a smile for days. 'Only you have ever forced me to resort to bullying tactics.'

'Because I won't let you walk all over me.'

'Because you never know when to give up!' he snapped, then glanced briefly at her and sighed. 'Look, you are tired, I am tired. And—dammit, Marnie, but I can still remember the last time I trusted you to remain where I left you only to find you had disappeared within an hour of my leaving you! And I have no intention of suffering another six months like those again,' he said grimly.

So, he'd suffered: good. So had she. He deserved to. She did not. She felt no pangs of sympathy, no twinges of remorse for worrying him as she had. Her own sorrow had been much harder to shut out. Guy had not held the monopoly on distress.

On her return to London there had been plenty of people more than ready to tell her how much he had suffered during her absence, how Roberto had found it necessary to take back control of the company while his son went demented trying to find her. How Guy had, on drawing a blank with every avenue he tried, turned to the bottle instead and for weeks refused to listen to reason while he drowned his suffering in whisky.

Only when she had felt able to face the world again had she come out of hiding. And she had made Guy aware of her return in the most fitting way possible: with a legal notification that she had filed for divorce.

He had ranted, he had raved, he'd threatened her, and eventually, when he'd come to accept that nothing he could do was going to change her mind, he'd left her alone.

But he had continued to refuse to agree to a divorce. 'I will pay any penance you consider due to you, Marnie, with good grace,' he'd told her grimly. 'But not by taking back the vows I made to you. Those will stay, no matter what you say.'

'I say I will never be your wife again,' she'd told him bluntly. 'Which leaves us both living in a state of limbo if you continue to be stubborn about this.'

'Then limbo it has to be,' he agreed. 'But no divorce. It is an unarguable fact that time eventaully heals all wounds. You will forgive me one day, Marnie. We will stay in limbo until that day arrives.'

And they would have done, if Marnie had not played her final trump card. 'Sign the papers, Guy, or I will change the plea to adultery, citing Anthea, and drag the whole mucky thing through the courts in the most public way I can manage.'

He had signed. They both knew what her threat would do to his father if she carried it out, and Guy had just not been prepared to risk calling her bluff on it...

The car drew to a halt, and Marnie blinked, bringing her own wandering mind to a halt also, finding herself in the once familiar dimness of the basement car park to his private block of luxury apartments.

'Out,' Guy said, snapping open his own seatbelt and climbing lithely out of the low-slung car. Doing the same, Marnie stretched her tension-locked muscles while he moved to the boot and collected his suitcase.

They rode the lift to the penthouse floor in silence, neither apparently prepared to risk another row by making eye-contact, which seemed to be all it took to give the tension buzzing between them cause to vent itself.

Nothing really changes, Marnie thought ruefully to herself as she followed him into the apartment. Everything looked very much as it had done the last time she had been here. Oh, no doubt the walls had enjoyed a fresh lick of paint, she allowed, but other than that it felt a bit like walking through a time warp coming back here.

She shivered delicately.

'You know the layout,' Guy said. 'Take your pick of the guest rooms. I'll just get rid of this case...' He was already striding down the wide caramel and cream hallway towards the master bedroom. 'Be an angel, Marnie,' he called over his shoulder. 'See what Mrs Dukes has left in the fridge for dinner, will you?'

'You still have Mrs Dukes?' she asked in surprise. The prune-faced housekeeper had worked for Guy long before Marnie arrived on the scene.

He stopped, turning to mock her with a cynical look. 'Not everyone finds me as objectionable as you do, you know,' he drawled, and moved on, leaving her feeling ever so thoroughly put down.

She found a ready cooked chicken *cacciatore* sitting in the fridge with detailed instructions on how to heat it placed neatly on top of the dish.

That made Marnie smile, despite her mood. Neither she nor Guy was much use in the kitchen, and Mrs Dukes had a habit of leaving precise instructions on how not to ruin her carefully prepared dishes.

Marnie followed the instructions to the letter, gaining some childish kind of pleasure in mockingly checking each command as it came up on the list. Mrs Dukes was a quiet, aloof kind of woman. Nice, but not someone Marnie had ever felt she could get close to. The housekeeper had always considered the kitchen her domain. And if she and Guy ever had ventured in here in the dead of night to pillage the fridge, they had used to do it like two naughty children. Mrs Dukes' kitchen, they'd used to call it. Mrs Dukes' cooker. Mrs Dukes' fridge.

A sharp pang of something she had no wish to acknowledge pulled her up short and she walked quickly out of the room, turning towards the guest bedrooms in search of the room she would be using tonight. Only her feet slowed outside another door. The door to her old studio. A room she had not entered since the night four years ago when she'd flown at Guy.

If the kitchen had been Mrs Dukes' domain, then this, Marnie recalled, had been hers. North-facing, wide-windowed and converted exclusively to suit her needs. Guy had provided her with every conceivable artistic aid she could possibly require.

Slowly, almost unsure that she actually wanted to do it, she turned the handle and stepped quietly inside.

It was empty. Her heart gave a painful dive. The room was bare, completely stripped of everything that had once been so familiar to her. Weak tears beginning to cloud her vision, she moved slowly to the middle of the room.

All gone. Everything. Her easel from where it used to stand by the window, the draughtsman's board from close by where she worked for hours on her sketches before turning her attention to a canvas. The canvases themselves, rows of them which used to lean, face turned inwards to the walls, all gone. Things she had loved too much to sell but had never quite got around to hanging on the walls.

She had painted Guy in this room. He had stood—just there. Her misty gaze went to the spot on the polished floor where he had posed naked for her in that oh, so arrogant way of his. 'Like this?' he'd teased her, turning his impressive body into some disgustingly provoking pose or other. 'Or this perhaps?' taking up another pose which would verge on the indecent while she tried to remain professional and shift him into a more respectable position. 'How am I supposed to stand here calmly dressed like this?' he'd demanded when she'd scolded him.

'You aren't dressed in anything!' she'd laughingly pointed out.

'Neither will you be in a minute,' he'd growled.

Now there was nothing left in the room but the echoes, echoes of something warm and special...

'I had the room cleared when it became—obvious that you had no intention of coming back to me,' a deep voice murmured from the doorway, making her spin round to find him standing there with his dark eyes guarded. 'I thought, for a time,' he went on quietly, 'that you might have at least wanted your canvases, but...' His shrug said all the rest, leaving a heavy silence behind it.

Marnie blinked away the mists from her eyes. 'W-what did you do with them?'

'Put them into store.' Another shrug. 'They are at Oaklands. Everything.' His gaze drifted around the bare emptiness of the room. 'The lot.'

She just hadn't been able to bear the idea of coming in here again to get anything. Not the tools of her trade or even her precious paintings.

'Still,' Guy went on more briskly, 'you can set up shop again at Oaklands once we've settled in there—so long as you don't take in any outside work, that is. Did you find anything to eat in the kitchen?'

Just like that. The subject of her continuing to work, opened and closed, just like that. Her mouth tightened, any hint of softening in her mood gone. 'A chicken *cacciatore*,' she answered coolly. 'Ready in about fifteen minutes.'

'Good.' He nodded. 'That will give us time to take a quick shower before we eat,' he decided, levering himself away from the door-frame. 'Have you decided which room you want to use?'

'It's all the same to me, since there is nothing here I relate to any more,' she answered bitterly. Then, because she did not feel she had the energy for a return to hostilities, she added flatly, 'I'll use the one next door to yours, if it's all the same to you.'

'But it isn't all the same to me,' he grunted. 'And you know it.' She glared at him and he sighed heavily. 'All right, Marnie. Use what bloody room you want to use. You know Mrs Dukes; she will have left them all prepared ready for unexpected guests.'

'I need a change of clothes,' she reminded him as he turned to leave. 'I suppose there's no chance you have any of my old things hanging around?' she enquired hopefully.

'No,' he muttered. 'If you must know, I had them sent to your favourite charity—at least that should please you, since nothing else around here seems to!'

'You gave all my lovely clothes to the Sally Army?' she choked out disbelievingly.

'What the hell did you expect me to do with them—have them lovingly preserved behind glass just in case you decided on a whim to come and collect them?'

'No, of course not!' she answered stiffly. 'I just thought...' Her voice trailed off. She didn't know what she'd thought—or even if she had so much as wondered about her clothes before this moment. 'It—it doesn't matter.' Dully she dropped the subject.

Guy seemed happy to do that too, because he nodded grimly and said, 'I will get you a pair of my pyjamas and a spare bathrobe. Tomorrow, first thing, we will go and collect your things from your flat, if that makes you feel any better.'

And he disappeared down the hall, his movements sharp with irritation. She followed, passing his door to open the one next to it, feeling as though she'd been dragged through the emotional food-mixer, the way they had to constantly keep sniping at each other.

Oh, God. She sat down wearily on the bed. What was she doing, letting herself become trapped by him again? She knew it could only lead to more heartache. More wretched pain. She was in pain now—the constant nagging pain of forced remembrance. Being with him all the time like this was making her face all those things she had thrust so utterly to the back of her mind.

Good things as well as bad. And she wasn't at all sure which side of the balance-scale was weighing down the heaviest. That frightened her, frightened because it had to mean that her grievances towards Guy were slowly beginning to fade away—just as he had always said they would do.

'Here. I've brought you...'

Guy halted a stride inside the room, his words dying as he looked down at her pale, forlorn face.

'Oh, Marnie,' he sighed, his mouth taking on a grim downward turn as he came over to where she sat and threw down the pyjamas and robe before squatting on his haunches in front of her. He took up her hands, long-fingered and so slender-boned that you only had to look at them to know they belonged to someone who possessed special artistic gifts. They were cold and trembling, and Guy sighed again before he lifted them to his lips and gently kissed them. He had discarded his jacket somewhere, and his tie, so the tanned skin at his throat where he had yanked open the top button of his shirt gleamed smoothly in the dying sunlight.

'Can't you simply forgive?' he murmured suddenly. 'Put us both out of our wretched misery and forgive so we can at least try to move forward into a better understanding than all this bitter standing still?'

She looked down into his face—so handsome, so sleekly hewn beneath its smooth, dark skin. His eyes, dark and deep, lacking any hint of mockery or cynicism or even the impatience he had been showing her all day. And his mouth, grim but soft, not tight and hard. Unhappy, like hers. Weary, like hers.

'I'll—try,' she whispered thickly, then sucked in a breath of air that entered her lungs like a shaky sigh, the tears she had been trying to hold back since she entered her old studio minutes ago suddenly bulging in her eyes.

Guy's mouth moved on a grimace of sombre understanding. And he lifted one of his hands to gently stroke her long bright hair away from the single tear trailing down her pale cheek. He made no effort to wipe the tear away, but simply squatted there watching its downward path until it reached the corner of her trembling mouth, when he leaned forward and gently kissed it away.

'I ask for nothing more,' he murmured gruffly. 'Nothing more.'

Marnie made an effort to gather herself, pulling her hands free and sitting up straighter on the bed, effectively putting much needed distance between them, both on a physical and a spiritual plane.

'The chicken will be ruined,' she said, trying for a rueful smile.

'Not if we're quick,' he countered, taking his lead from her and straightening his long body into a standing position. 'A quick shower each, and we'll meet in the kitchen in five minutes.' He turned to walk back to the door—then stopped, turning back to glance around the room.

'This is all right for you?' he asked politely.

Marnie stood up. 'Yes,' she said uninterestedly. 'It's fine.'

'You . . .' He lifted a hand to run it through his hair in a oddly uncertain gesture. 'Would you prefer to use our old room while I use this one?'

The action and his curious tone made her frown. 'No,' she refused. 'That's your room. You'll sleep better in your own bed. Of course I don't want to take it from you.'

'Sleep?' he murmured drily. 'What's that?' The hand moved to the back of his neck, holding it while he grimaced wryly at her. 'I have not had a single moment's sleep since you came back into my life two nights ago,' he admitted. 'I just lie there, listening to every move you make, on the alert in case you decide to make a bolt for it again.'

'I told you I wouldn't,' she reminded him.

'I know.' The hand dropped heavily to his side and clenched into a fist. 'But it makes no difference. What is it that keeps you awake, Marnie?' he then posed softly.

You, she wanted to say. Memories. My own black thoughts. 'I give you my solemn vow, Guy,' she said drily instead, 'that I will not move out of this bed once I am in it—will that help ease your fractious mind?'

'No.' He smiled. 'But I suppose it will have to do. See you in five minutes.' Then he was gone, leaving her feeling ever so slightly—perplexed.

They ate in silence, Marnie with the long sleeves of his pyjama top rolled over several times before she found her hands. He'd grinned at the sight of her when she'd first walked into the kitchen but had said nothing, the small compromise she had allowed seeming to have taken all the tension out of the air. The chicken was not quite ruined, the pasta still edible, just about, and they washed it down with a glass of good Italian white wine.

Not very long after they had finished the meal, Marnie yawned and got up, more than ready for her bed.

She only hoped she could manage to sleep a little tonight. Certainly she was more than tired enough to do so.

And thankfully she did, dropping off to sleep almost as soon as her head hit the pillow, curling herself into a loose ball with the feel of Guy's pyjamas cocooning her in sensual silk. In fact, the feeling was so provocative that she found herself drifting into an erotic dream, where Guy was no longer her enemy and she was welcoming him into her bed and her arms as though he had never left them.

He felt wonderful to the touch, his skin like fine leather beneath her exploring fingertips, her mouth automatically softening as he gently kissed her.

'Mmm,' she sighed out pleasurably.

'Go back to sleep,' he murmured.

Back to sleep——? Her eyes flew open, her heart beginning to race madly when she found herself securely curled into the warm curve of his body.

'What are you doing here?' she gasped, trying to pull away.

He wouldn't let her. 'Don't start, Marnie.' He sighed out wearily. 'I have not come here to seduce you, if that is what you are thinking.'

'Then why are you here?' she demanded, glaring coldly at him as he reluctantly opened his eyes.

'I still couldn't sleep. So I decided the next best option was to join you here. As a therapy, it is working,' he yawned, his eyes closing sleepily. 'I am almost dead to the world already.'

'But—Guy!' she cried, managing to get an arm free and flinging it out to grab hold of his shoulder. It felt like satin beneath her touch, warm and tightly muscled. 'Guy!' she snapped, giving him a shake.

But he was already asleep! She couldn't believe it! Could not believe his utter gall in just calmly climbing into bed with her. She sighed angrily, gave the satin shoulder a mulish slap and sighed again, letting her head fall back on to the pillow because, fast asleep or not, he was still holding on to her, giving her no room to escape.

'If you're kidding me with this stupid game, I'll kill you, Guy Frabosa!' she muttered, watching his relaxed face for any hint that he was just feigning sleep.

His breathing was light and even, his mouth parted slightly and relaxed, eyes closed so the silken brush of his long dark lashes lay in a perfect arch across his high cheekbones.

She studied him closely for long, suspicious minutes, his face bare inches away from her own, waiting for the slightest hint that he was only waiting for her to relax before he pounced. But he hardly moved, his body completely relaxed beneath the soft warm duvet, and as the minutes ticked by her own body became used to having his wound so intimately around it, legs tangled, the comforting feel of his arms folded so possessively around her, her breasts brushing lightly against his chest as she breathed.

The only man ever to hold her like this, she thought sadly. Guy. The man she loved to hate and hated to love.

'Why do you still do this to me?' she whispered to his sleeping face. 'Why does this feel so right?'

She sighed softly, her eyes full of a kind of tender tragedy as she closed the few small inches between them and gently kissed him on the mouth. He did not respond; was too deeply asleep to have even noticed.

Sighing again, she relaxed back on to the pillows, her expression open and vulnerable as she continued to watch him sleep in her arms until slowly her own eyes began to droop, her body growing heavy until it relaxed tiredly into his.

Then she too slept.

The morning wasn't so easy to accept when she awoke to find herself still curled cosily into his warm body. She opened her eyes to find his brown ones watching her lazily.

'This is nice.' Guy obviously felt no qualms about voicing what she was guiltily thinking. 'I did consider waking the Sleeping Beauty with a kiss,' he teased her wryly. 'But I am afraid I feared the reprisals.'

She droped her gaze from his, then wished she hadn't when her gaze fell on to her hand, still lovingly curled around his satin shoulder. Carefully, she removed it, then let it hover, not knowing quite what to do with it now, since the only other places she could rest it involved the warm flesh of the man lying beside her.

'Here.' Reaching out, he took the hand in his own, his fingers closing around hers as he brought them up to his mouth to brush a light kiss against them then folded them beneath the duvet into the narrow gap between their bodies. 'Do you know how peacefully you sleep?' he murmured questioningly. 'You barely move, barely breathe—I used to lie watching you for hours, you know,' he confessed, 'envying you that blissful peace.'

'You're too over-active-minded to sleep with any hope of peace,' she threw back drily, smiling, despite her discomfort with the situation.

'Over-active other parts of me as well, if I recall,' he teased.

Marnie blushed and quickly changed the subject. 'You have more of these,' she noted, freeing her captured hand so she could comb a finger through the silvered hairs at his temple.

'My father was completely grey by his fiftieth birthday,' he informed her, sounding gruffly defensive suddenly.

Marnie glanced into his guarded eyes. 'It wasn't a criticism,' she told him quietly, realising where the defensiveness had come from. 'I like the silver. I always did. It makes you look so distinguished. I like Roberto's hair, too,' she added quickly to defuse any hint of intimacy he might have read into the remark. 'It makes *him* look distinguished.'

Guy just smiled, moving his gaze to her own hair, lying like a rippling red-gold stream out across the pillow behind her. Reaching over her, he picked up a silken tendril and brought it to his face, his eyelids lowering as he inhaled the rose-scented smell of it in a way which made her stomach curl. Guy could always make the simplest gesture seem so exquisitely sensual.

The heavy lids lifted again, catching her expression. 'I...' she floundered, not sure what she wanted to say, not sure if there was anything she could say to stop what was actually beginning to happen between them.

His own eyes darkened, his hand moving to her shoulder, and slowly, giving her more than enough time to realise what he intended to do, he gently pushed her on to her back, then came to lean over her.

'Say no, if you want to,' he murmured huskily, then brought his mouth down warmly on to hers.

CHAPTER EIGHT

THE night's stubble on Guy's chin rasped lightly against Marnie's more sensitive flesh. Their warm bodies gravitated instinctively towards one another; her limbs parted to accommodate him, and Guy obliged by covering her completely, sending a thrill of pleasure rushing through her as she languidly accepted his weight.

The kiss went on and on, neither deepening nor receding. No tangled tongues, no desperate surge of passion to force her to make the unwanted decision as to whether she let them continue further down the road to ultimate union.

It was as though they were content to just recapture a poignant moment from the past when they could exchange kisses like this, warm, tender, giving kisses that did not necessarily need to tumble into the heated fire of sensuality to give satisfaction.

Marnie lifted her hands to his throat, then slid them to his nape, her fingers burying themselves in the jet-dark mass of his hair.

Guy let out a short, breathy sigh, and tangled his own hands in her hair, cupping her head, lifting her closer to him, his body beginning to move slightly, just the merest hint of a thrusting rhythm that made her stomach clench and begin to churn.

She wasn't sure whose mouth parted first, or whose tongue went in sensual search of the other, but suddenly their mouths were straining, the kiss becoming heated, their breathing agitated enough to make them both move restlessly against each other. She felt the hardened thrust of his arousal, gasped and arched as it moved pleasurably against her.

'Guy,' she whispered feverishly.

'Ssh,' he said, sliding his moist mouth across her cheek to begin sucking seductively at her earlobe, while his hand slid between their bodies, finger sliding buttons free, parting her top so he could bring his chest back down upon her naked skin.

He sighed tremulously as she responded to the new delight of flesh against flesh, and brought his mouth back to hers, warm and seductive, his hands moving on further down until they were gently kneading her soft flesh as his hips thrust insistently against her own.

Moisture began to spring out all over his skin, musky-scented and so familiar to her that she groaned in pleasure as it assailed her nostrils. Her fingertips dug in as they ran from muscle-packed shoulders down the full length of his long back until they reached his waist, where they slid sideways, making him shudder, his muscles jerking in spasm as she searched out his acutely sensitive groin, cupping the rigid bones in his hips with her palms while her fingers moved incitingly.

And, as if her joining in the sensual foreplay he had begun was like giving leave for him to do his worst to her, Guy gasped something and slid his hand inside her pyjama bottoms so he could push them out of his way.

Marnie felt something buried deep inside her crack, and like a dam with its seams burst open wide all her long-suppressed passions came flooding through, sending her arching towards that knowing hand, and on a husky groan she bit sensually down into his lower lip, making him start, jerk away from her to gaze hotly down into her flushed face. The mayhem going on inside her must have shown in the passionate glitter in her eyes, because Guy muttered something beneath his breath, and tried shakily to calm her.

'I hate what you do to me!' she choked out wretchedly.

'No, you don't,' he denied, stroking a shaking hand across her flaming hair in an odd gesture of sympathy. 'You only wish you did, my darling,' he murmured, and brought his mouth back on to her before she could say another bitter word, burning her with a kiss that banished every other feeling from her but the hungry need to touch and feel.

His caresses grew urgent, more intimate, giving her no opportunity to return to the sanity she had let go of, his mouth sliding down her body to nip, lick and kiss her into a frenzy of desire. Her breathing was out of control, rasping hectically from her lips as he took one of her thrusting breasts into his mouth and sucked hard, until the pain of it became a terrible pleasure.

'You want me,' he said hoarsely, knowing her body better than she even did herself.

'Yes,' she answered, not even sorry to admit it any more.

'How much?' He ran his tongue across the recently abused tip of her breast, its newly heightened sensitivity making her cry out in pleasure.

She didn't answer. Her teeth clenched tightly against her searing breath to stop the words he wanted to hear escaping through.

His hot breath burned her where it brushed, his body, slick with sweat, moving with a slow eroticism against her, arousing her with the sensual experience of a man who knew his own power.

Barely able to breathe as that slow, desperate build-up of feeling began to grow within the centre of her, she could feel herself beginning to float, her limbs tightening, her mind losing itself in the dizzy mists of sexual ecstasy.

'How much?' he demanded again.

Heart, body and soul. He wanted to hear her repeat the husky little love chant he had forced from her every time they made love before. But——

She shook her head. 'No,' she refused again, sane enough to know she could not give him more than she was already giving him. Desperate enough to sob at her own strength to refuse him this one simple but oh, so telling little phrase. 'Never again,' she whispered wretchedly. 'Never again, Guy, never again.'

'The heated throb of your body says you want me,' he muttered. 'It pulses with a need to feel me filling you inside! Your soul cries out for reunion with mine—I can hear it, even now while you lie here beneath me trying to deny its right to belong! I can hear it, Marnie, calling out to mine! And your heart.' He covered her left breast where her heart pumped heavily against his resting hand. 'What does this wildly pulsating heartbeat tell me?'

'It tells you nothing—nothing!' she cried, finding enough strength to push him away from her and rolling dizzily off the bed to stand. 'I wonder sometimes if you're some kind of throwback from the Dark Ages,' she muttered, hugging her trembling body because she had a terrible feeling it was going to shatter if she didn't. 'How dare you expect more from me than you're capable of giving yourself?'

He was lying where she had left him, on his back in all his arrogant nakedness, his expression grimly closed. 'I gave you everything of myself the day we married,' he stated coolly.

Marnie let out a deriding sound, dragging the flaps of her top around her aching breasts and trying to pretend that she didn't give a damn that he had managed to bring her tumbling back to her senses before the whole thing had spun way out of control. 'And Anthea?' she threw at him bitterly. 'What was she supposed to be—a moment's loss of sanity?'

He nodded. 'You could call her that,' he agreed. 'But, as I said to you only the other day, Anthea is a part of the past and is no longer up for discussion. It is over——'

'Gone, forgotten, I know,' she finished for him. 'Well,' she snapped, 'so are the promises from the past. If you want my full commitment to you a second time, then you will have to earn it a second time.' Jerkily she moved across the room to the adjoining bathroom door. 'Now get off my bed, and out of my room,' she told him as she tugged open the door. 'The right to enter either is not yours quite yet!'

Slamming the bathroom door shut behind her and locking it, Marnie then leaned back against the solid safety of the wood and closed her eyes.

She hated him! Hated! she told herself fiercely.

But a lump formed in her aching throat, put there by the guilty knowledge that, even while she did hate, she wanted him with a hunger that was growing stronger with each hour she spent in his company. And if he hadn't pushed his luck too far just now, then she would be still lying beneath him, glorying in the pleasure only Guy could give her.

Emerging half an hour later, Marnie made directly for the sitting-room with the intention of using the telephone extension in there. But she was brought up short for a moment when she found Guy lounging on one of the soft-cushioned sofas reading his daily newspaper.

He didn't look up, and, lifting her chin in outright defiance at the sudden hungry jolt her senses gave her, she marched over to the phone and picked it up.

'What are you doing?' Guy enquired lazily.

'Ringing Jamie,' she told him, holding the receiver to her ear. 'I want to know how Clare is, and if——'

'They're not there,' he said coolly, flipping over a newspaper sheet.

'Not there?' Alarm skittered down her spine. 'Why?' she gasped. 'Is it Clare? Is she——?'

'Of course not!' he sighed. 'So stop letting that wild imagination of yours run away with you. Clare is fine.'

'Then why are you so certain they won't be at the garage?' she demanded. 'It's Saturday. Jamie is open on a Saturday. He——'

'They are not your concern any more,' Guy inserted levelly. 'Leave them to get on with their own lives.'

'Not my concern? Of course they're my concern!' she snapped. 'They're my family!'

'I am the only family you need concern yourself about from now on.'

'No way!' Marnie shook her bright head. 'I've willingly given up everything else for you, Guy. I will not give up my family as well!'

'Willingly?' he quizzed, lifting his dark head from his newspaper to mock her with a look.

'Willingly or unwillingly,' she snapped. 'What difference does it make? I've done it. But Jamie and Clare are all I have left, and I won't let you take them away from me, too!'

'You have me,' he pointed out.

But I don't want you! she wanted to tell him, but held the words back, snapping her lips shut over her clenched teeth as she turned her attention back to the telephone again. No answer; she let it ring and ring, then, in the end, placed the receiver slowly back on its rest and turned to look at Guy.

'What have you done with them, Guy?' she demanded huskily.

'Done?' He glanced at her with amusement spiking his eyes, then away again. 'That is charming,' he scoffed. 'Are you suspecting me of some dastardly crime, Marnie?' he mocked. 'Like spiriting them away to some wretched place and doing them in?'

'Don't be stupid!' she snapped. Then, doubtfully, 'What have you done with them?'

He sighed, his eyes flicking impatiently over the newspaper sheets as if he was intending not to answer. Then he said flatly, 'They are not at the garage because they are at Oaklands. Your brother is working for me again. He and Clare moved into the Lodge House by the West Gate yesterday.'

'Jamie—working back at Oaklands?' Her voice mirrored her shocked disbelief. Her brother had always vowed never to work for anyone but himself again. 'But why? How——?'

'Why?' Guy drawled sardonically. 'Because he is not fit to run his own business. And how? By doing as he was told and transporting himself, his charming wife, his impressive collection of tools—and my MG Magnette—down to Oaklands the day after he talked you into taking the rap for his own sins.'

'My God.' Stunned at how quickly he had turned all their lives inside out, she sank weakly into a nearby chair. 'You mean—you took them over, lock, stock and barrel, just like that?'

'Just like that,' he agreed. 'Let's call it—protecting my investment,' he smiled. 'With your brother and his wife solely reliant on my goodwill to keep food on their plates and a roof over their heads, I should have no problem keeping my feisty wife in order.'

But her mind was too busy working overtime even to care about his provoking sarcasm. There was more to all of this than Guy was actually telling her—or her brother if she was reading her prickling instincts correctly. 'And the garage?' she questioned narrowly. 'What is to become of that?'

'That now belongs to me,' he said. 'And it goes up for sale first thing Monday morning.'

'How much?' she then demanded grimly. 'How much exactly does my brother owe you?'

He ignored the question, seemingly engrossed in an article he was reading. Blue eyes beginning to burn, Marnie got up and stepped over to flick at the wretched newspaper he was so interested in with her hand. 'How much?' she demanded.

Guy took his time bringing his head up to look at her, and when he did there was more than just a mild warning in his eyes. 'None of your damned business,' he enunciated slowly. 'If I was stupid enough to let him tap me for money, then that is my affair, not yours.'

'But——'

'Drop it, Marnie!' he ground out suddenly, thrusting the newspaper aside and surging to his feet. 'Just drop it before I get really angry, which I could very easily do, the way I feel right now. So be warned!'

'No,' she refused, taking hold of his arm as he went to stride away. 'Guy, please tell me just how deeply we are in your debt.'

'Enough to keep you in line, Marnie, never fear,' he derided.

'Oh, God.' White-faced, she sank down on the sofa where Guy had just been sitting. 'I had no idea,' she whispered. 'Jamie never uttered a single word that he'd been borrowing money from you of his own volition.'

His mouth tightened at her obvious distress. 'Look,' he sighed. 'If it makes you feel any better about it, it was Jamie who suggested he come back to Oaklands to work for me. And it was he who offered his garage to me as collateral against the money he owes me. He's learning, Marnie,' he added grimly. 'Learning to take responsibility for his own life at last. Let him be. Let him do it. He has used you and me and what we feel for each other for quite long enough.'

'And Clare?' she whispered thickly. 'Is she to be cast out in the cold also?'

'No one,' Guy said heavily, 'is being cast out! Only made to bear the brunt of their own actions. And if you think about it, Marnie,' he added quietly, 'Clare will be living a mere stone's throw away from you from now on. Surely that makes it easier for you to cosset her, not less? Now,' he said briskly 'let's get over to your flat. I want to be at Oaklands before sundown.'

He drove her to her flat in an atmosphere of grim silence, Marnie's thoughts locked on the shocked discovery that her brother had even dared to approach Guy for money on his own! And Guy, she wondered frowningly. What had driven him to so much as give a penny to a man he liked to blame his broken marriage on?

You know the answer, a little voice said inside her head. He did it because of you.

He had never been inside her flat before. She went off to her bedroom to change into fresh underwear and a short straight apple-green silk skirt which had its own matching loosely cut jacket, and a white silk blouse before turning her attention to her packing.

She could hear Guy moving about in her studio-cum-sitting-room, arrogantly fishing around her private possessions as if he had the right. Her mouth tightened, resentment at his presumptuousness sending her stalking around her bedroom collecting and throwing her clothes into her open suitcases with scant regard to how they were going to look when she unpacked them again.

He was standing viewing her latest painting when she emerged, his dark head tilted to one side in interested study.

'This is good,' he said without turning to look at her. 'Who is it?'

'Amelia Sangster,' she answered shortly. Then couldn't help adding with a smile in her voice, 'And the cat's name is Dickens.'

'Heavy name for such a sweet little cat,' he mocked.

'He doesn't think so.' Marnie walked over to stand beside him. 'He sleeps every night curled up on Amelia's leather-bound volumes of Dickens' full works—— Will I be allowed to deliver this?' she asked shortly. 'Or is poor Amelia to be disappointed like all my other expectant clients?'

Guy turned his head to look down at her, his expression telling her absolutely nothing as he searched her cool face. She had left her hair down this morning, and the waving tresses shimmered around her face and shoulders, lit by the sunlight seeping in through the window.

'Is it finished?' he asked.

'Can't you tell?' she drawled sarcastically, refusing point-blank to admit that the picture was so close to being finished that probably only an expert eye would be able to tell it wasn't. And Guy had never professed to being an art expert.

He ignored the sarcasm. 'Do you want to finish it?'

'Of course!' she snapped, amazed that he should even have to ask such a stupid question.

He just shrugged. 'Then I will have it picked up and delivered to Oaklands,' he said. 'But the rest——' he lifted his right hand up so she could see the big black appointments book he was holding '—will have to stay disappointed.'

'But—that's my appointments book!' she exclaimed. 'What are you doing with it?'

'Holding on to it for future reference,' he drawled.

'Future reference to what?'

'To all those poor people we are going to disappoint,' he answered with maddening calm. 'I will have my secretary write them all a nice letter, letting them down gently.'

'I can do that myself,' she clipped, reaching out to take the book.

He moved it smoothly out of her way. 'No, you won't,' he murmured, returning his attention back to Amelia and her cat. 'I don't trust you, Marnie,' he informed her quite casually, 'to do what is needed to be done. So I will pass the job on to my very reliable secretary.'

'God, I despise you,' she muttered, moving away from him.

He shrugged as if that didn't matter to him either. 'Packed everything you need?' he enquired.

'Yes.' Suddenly she felt like weeping, coming to a standstill in the middle of the cluttered studio and gazing around her like a child about to lose everything that was comfortable and secure in its life.

She'd been happy here—if happiness could be gauged by the gentle waves of peace and contentment she had managed to surround herself with. Like an island, she realised. Living here alone for the last four years had been like living on a tranquil island, after spending a year in the ruthless jungle Guy existed in.

'Then the rest can be delivered along with the painting,' Guy decided. 'Show me where your cases are and let's get going.'

The tears remained clogging the back of her throat as she watched Guy lift her suitcases and carry them to the door. Once there, he turned back to find her standing there, her face white with misery.

'Guy——?' she whispered pleadingly, but what she was pleading for Marnie just did not know.

His face darkened, his expression suddenly fierce as he spun away from her. 'I'll take these down to the car,' he muttered, and walked out, leaving her standing there, feeling about as lost and helpless as she had ever felt in her whole life.

He didn't come back, and Marnie knew why. He was waiting for her to go to him. If he had to come back and drag her out, then it would mean that she was still fighting him for every inch of herself she could keep. If she walked out of the flat of her own accord, then he'd won another small battle. Small, because they both knew she really had no choice.

He was sitting with the car window rolled down, his arm resting on it, his long fingers lying along the thin line of his mouth. He looked darkly handsome and grimly forbidding with his profile turned to her like that, and she felt her heart squeeze on a final clutch of regret at what she was leaving behind.

He didn't turn his head to look at her as she closed the main door to the Victorian town-house her flat was a part of. Or bother to watch her walk to the car and around it to climb into the passenger seat beside him. Neither did he move while she settled herself, locking home her safety-belt, flicking back her hair from her pale face. When she finally went still, he straightened in his seat, reached out to start the engine, pressed a button which sent his window sliding smoothly upwards, then slid the car into gear.

Marnie swallowed, keeping her own eyes staring bleakly frontwards. They moved into the traffic. And, as they left the flat as she had called home for four blessed years, she finally accepted that her life would never be her own again.

Guy owned it now.

Perhaps more solidly than he had done the first time around.

'What now?' she managed to ask once she felt she had her voice under control.

'Now, we begin,' he said, and that was all, the words simple but profound.

CHAPTER NINE

IT WAS a perfect time to be arriving at Oaklands. They entered by the East Gate late afternoon, as the June sun hovered high above the hilltop opposite.

'Guy—stop a moment,'

He glanced questioningly at her, his eyes darkened as he brought the car to a halt and turned to watch the enchantment light her face.

'I always loved this place,' she murmured, unaware of just how much of her inner self she was revealing with that wistfully spoken statement. 'Oh, look, Guy!' she cried, leaning forward in her eagerness. 'The stream is swollen so wide it could almost be a river!'

'The weather has been poor in the hills for this time of year,' he told her, his gaze remaining fixed on her rapt profile. 'There was a time a few weeks ago when we worried it might burst its banks.'

'I can see that the lake is full, too,' she said, gazing down to where the water lapped the rim of the rickety old jetty where Roberto's small rowing-boat bobbed gently up and down.

The house was there. Big and solid and sure. Standing as it had done for two centuries, surviving everything the years had thrown at it through a succession of owners, not all of them kind to its sturdy walls.

'You've made some changes over there,' she noticed, pointing towards the stable block where, just beyond and to the right, her artistic eye for detail had picked out a new addition. A small building that looked like a cottage, built to blend graciously in with its present surroundings. 'A new annexe for your cars?' she supposed, frowning because it seemed a long way from the other buildings where Guy housed his precious collection.

'Something like that,' he answered unrevealingly, then put the car in motion again. 'My father will have already spotted us coming in the gates,' he said. 'If we don't drive down there soon, he will be striding up here to meet us!'

'W-what have you told him?'

Guy glanced at her, and saw she had gone pale, even with the warmth of the sun on her face. 'That we are reconciled,' he said, returning his attention back to the road. 'He is, as you would expect, ecstatic about it.' He sounded a trifle cynical. 'And I would prefer it, Marnie, if he remain that way.'

'Of course!' she cried, hurt that Guy should feel it necessary to warn her like that. 'You know I would never do anything to hurt your father!'

'You hurt him when you left us,' Guy reminded her.

'That was different,' she said uncomfortably. 'Roberto knows I still adore him.'

'I once believed you adored me, too. And look where it got me.'

'It got you what you deserved!' Marnie flashed. 'And I would think your father knows it!'

'You are probably right,' Guy ruefully agreed, slowing to guide the car deftly over the narrow little bridge which spanned the stream. 'Still,' he shrugged, 'he likes to kid himself that I am a son to be proud of. It would be a shame to disillusion him too much.'

'Well, his disillusionment will not come from me,' Marnie stated coolly. 'It never did.'

After crossing the racing track, the driveway took a sharp bend to the left, taking them sailing through the thick cluster of majestic oaks which gave the estate its name, and around to the front of the house which faced south, so it could catch the full day's sun in its face, no matter what time of year it was.

Guy drew the car to a stop then turned to look at her. 'Ready?' he asked.

'Yes.' She nodded, but her insides were trembling as she climbed out of the car.

Guy came to join her, his hand slipping around her waist and firmly drawing her body closer to his side. Marnie stiffened a little, appalled by how violently her senses reacted.

'Relax!' he admonished. 'And turn your face and smile at me! Do it!' he whispered fiercely when she went to refuse. 'My father has just come out of the house and is watching us!'

Having to force it, Marnie turned her bright head, tilted her face and smiled up at him. Their eyes clashed, and held, the air around them suddenly too dense to breathe, when she felt something sting her sharply. She gasped. Guy went tense, his heartbeat quickening. And she felt her own begin to hammer, that strange imaginary sting sending tingling shock-waves outwards to every corner of her body. His irises darkened, spiralling out from rich liquid brown to deep black pits that seemed to be drawing her closer and closer.

'Marnie,' Guy whispered hoarsely.

'No.' She tried to deny what she knew was happening to both of them. But her voice held no strength, and, even as she mouthed the word, her tongue was coming out to run sensually around her parted lips.

She wanted him to kiss her, she realised with a small shock. She not only wanted it, her whole body was crying out for it. Begging for it. Needing it.

His hand moved, flattening against her spine so he could urge her around in front of him. Then she was pressed against the solid length of his body, and Guy was slowly bringing his mouth down to cover her own.

The world began to spin, her senses spiralling with it. The hand at her back urged her closer, bending her into a subtle arch which brought her thighs into quivering contact with his hard arousal. His other hand buried itself in her hair, cupping her head so he could deepen the kiss, and Marnie let her hands drift restlessly over his muscled arms until they fell heavily over his shoulders. Her breasts tightened, the stinging nubs pushing themselves against the warm hardness of his chest. Guy drew in a shaky breath and held on to it, his body beginning to tremble. She felt it just as her own began to do the same. And when he eventually dragged his mouth away from hers they both looked dazed, bewildered, heavy-eyed with need.

'Don't ever deny that we have this!' he rasped out thickly. 'No matter what else we lost, Marnie, we never lost this!'

He made to take her mouth again, but she pulled stiffly out of his arms, suddenly feeling so cold and empty inside that she shivered.

She moved away from him, swallowing in an effort to shift the lump from her throat, and struggling to pull herself together before turning her attention on the watchful Roberto Frabosa.

He looked older than the last time she'd seen him, and so infinitely frail, standing there with his tall, thin body leaning so elegantly on his walking stick, that she found it easy to discover her smile again, warm it, make it the most natural smile she had used in days.

'Papa,' she murmured, and began to move quickly towards him.

His free arm went tightly around her, his face burying itself into her hair for a long emotional moment before he said gruffly, 'This has to be the most beautiful moment of my life, Marnie. The most beautiful.'

He lifted his head, gazing at her with suspiciously moist eyes. 'Thank you,' she said simply.

'And it is all over now?' he demanded, glancing at his son as he came to join them. 'You love each other again?'

Love? Marnie's smile faltered. She didn't think she was capable of loving anyone again.

'The point is, Papa——' Guy's arm came possessively around her waist '—did we ever actually stop?'

'Well, you stopped doing something,' Roberto pointed out, 'or the last four years would not have been what they were!' He shook his silvered head. 'Barren years!' he condemned them impatiently. 'Such wasted, barren years!'

'Papa!' Guy's voice was unusually harsh as he felt Marnie jerk back against his arm as if she'd been shot.

'Take a small piece of advice from your son if you will——' with effort, he strained the harshness out of his voice but still sounded grim '—and resist the temptation to prod unstable substances. They tend to have this irritating tendency to explode in one's face!'

Marnie gasped at the unexpected outburst, and Roberto stared at Guy in sharp surprise. And in the ensuing silence which followed something passed between father and son over the top of Marnie's head that made Roberto go pale before he recovered, to send her a rueful smile.

'I have a cryptic for a son,' he mocked.

'Why did he snap at you like that?'

Marnie and Roberto were sitting alone in his private study, sipping coffee, surrounded by the precious books he spent most of his time poring over these days. Guy had disappeared as soon as good manners allowed, making for his workshops with all the eagerness of a young boy wanting to play with his favourite toys. Away in the distance she could hear the throaty roar of a car engine being revved experimentally, and could see in her mind's eye the circle of grease-covered bodies bent over the car listening with expert ears to the finely tuned sound.

When Guy had bought this private estate, some fifteen years ago now, he had done so with the intention of building his own racing track and workshops in the grounds. He had done all of this without managing to spoil the natural beauty of the surrounding valley, sparing no expense to achieve it, just as he would spare no expense to keep his precious collection in the very peak of its original condition.

He would, during their stay here, take each car out and put it through its paces, listen for faults, test its performance—but most of all enjoy himself—before railing at his mechanic if everything was not exactly as he expected it to be.

According to Roberto, the success of Guy's transition from world-class Grand Prix driver to high-powered businessman was entirely due to his having an outlet for his natural restlessness in his collection of cars.

He was a man of many faces, many moods. Quick to temper, quick to humour, and quick to passion. But for all that she had seen him curse and swear, laugh and tease, burn up with desire and seem to die in release, she had never seen him be anything but lovingly respectful to his father.

Roberto glanced sharply at her. 'You think I did not deserve my roasting?' he quizzed.

'No,' she answered. 'And it just isn't like him to speak to you like that.'

'But there you have just hit the nail unwittingly on its head, my dear,' Roberto said gravely. 'My son is not himself. And has not been for a long time. Four years, in fact.'

Marnie lowered her face, refusing to take him on with that one.

'I am a very proud and loving father, Marnie,' he went on coolly. 'But do not think me blind to his faults, for I am not.'

'Guy has no faults,' she mocked.

Roberto smiled at her joke, but shook his head in a refusal to be diverted. 'And I find myself wondering, you know, why, after all the pain and misery you have put each other through, you are now deciding to try again at a marriage which could not have been as good as it seemed the first time, for it to falter so totally at the first obstacle it came up against.'

But what an obstacle, Marnie thought, then glanced narrowly at Roberto. 'We don't do it for the sake of an old man, if that's what you're thinking,' she said shrewdly.

He nodded slowly. 'But maybe you do it for the sake of your brother?'

Her face stiffened, her body along with it. 'Not for him, either,' she said.

'Then maybe,' Roberto suggested silkily, 'you do it for that sweet angel of a wife your brother brought here with him yesterday?'

'You've seen Clare?' Marnie asked eagerly. 'How did she look? Did she look well? She's pregnant, you know, and she shouldn't be.' Her face clouded, aching concern showing in her blue eyes. 'She lost a baby a couple of months ago and the doctors warned her then that her body needed time to heal; I...'

'She is well, Marnie—very well,' Roberto reassured her gently. 'She spent the whole afternoon here with me, while your brother and Guy's team of mechanics moved their things into the lodge. She was happy, excited about the baby. Excited about the move to the country. Excited about the vacation her husband has taken her on for the next few weeks to get them over the—er—critical time.'

Vacation? Marnie's eyes sharpened. What vacation? Jamie couldn't afford to take a——

Guy. She sat back, not sure if she was angry or grateful to him for that piece of thoughtfulness. Then she realised this was yet another thing he had done of his own volition: showing thoughtfulness and caring where none had been requested.

She frowned, trying to work out why on the one hand he could cut her brother into little pieces with his tongue, then on the other do something as beautiful as this.

Because of you, a small voice said. He does it for you. Don't you know he would do anything to ease your troubles? You were worried about Clare's health, so he packed her off on a holiday so she could relax and be cosseted through the next vital month.

Then why am I sitting here, she challenged that voice, being blackmailed by him to do the last thing on this earth I want to do?

Is it? the silent voice asked.

She wriggled uncomfortably.

Roberto watched the changing expressions passing across her open face for a while, then made to get up. 'Come,' he said, using his ever-present stick to help him rise from the chair. 'I want to show you something. And it is best viewed in good light.' A hand wafted imperiously at her when she didn't immediately respond. 'Come, come!' he commanded. 'My son will not thank me for stealing his thunder on this, but I believe the moment is right and not worth wasting. So come.'

Marnie came reluctantly to her feet. 'Roberto, do you think it worth risking Guy's wrath a second time in one day?' she posed dubiously.

'Why, what are you afraid he will do to me?' His dark eyes began to twinkle. 'Beat me with my own walking stick?

'No.' She laughed, shaking her head ruefully. 'But on your own head be it if he tears you off another strip with his tongue!'

He just tucked her hand into the crook of his arm, and with a deft flick of his wrist set his walking stick in front of him and led them out through the French windows which opened on to a winding pathway that led through his many carefully pruned rose-beds.

'Where are we going?' she asked curiously.

'You will see soon enough,' he murmured secretively. 'Ah, but this is good,' he sighed. 'Walking the garden with a beautiful woman on my arm. I had forgotten just how good it can feel!'

'You old charmer,' Marnie teased, and reached over to kiss his leathery cheek.

'Now that,' he drawled, 'was even better!'

She laughed, and so did he, neither aware of how easily the sound of their laughter floated on the still air to where several men stood talking in a huddle.

A head came up, dark and sleek, standing head and shoulders above the rest. He pin-pointed the sound, frowned for a moment, then went back into the huddle, his concentration broken while he puzzled over what was eluding him.

'Oh——!' Marnie cried as they emerged through a small clump of trees into the evening sunlight again. 'How absolutely enchanting!'

In front of them, about a hundred feet away, stood the quaintest, sweetest little cottage she had ever seen. It could have been stolen right out of a child's picture story-book with its cream-washed walls clamouring with red and yellow roses.

'What is it?' she asked excitedly, realising that this must have been the building she'd picked out when she and Guy arrived on the estate. But she was at a complete loss as to why Guy would have constructed such a beautiful thing in this idyllic spot.

Then a sudden thought occurred to her and she turned sharply to her companion. 'Roberto?' she gasped. 'Is this for you? Have you decided to move out of the main house to live here?'

He just shook his head and refused to answer. 'Let us go inside,' he said, his smile enigmatic.

Letting him urge her forward again, Marnie found herself half expecting Little Miss Moffat sitting primly inside.

She could not have been more wrong, and stopped dead in her tracks, her breath suddenly imprisoned in her breast.

Not a cottage at all, her stunned mind was telling her, but a studio, a light and airy one-roomed studio made to look like a cottage from the outside so it could blend so perfectly with its surroundings.

They had come upon the place from the south, and really that sweet fairy-tale frontage was only a façade. The rest of the walls were wall-to-wall glass! Glass from the deep window-ledge that ran around the room from thigh-height onwards. And furnished with purely functional Venetian blinds, rolled away at the moment to let in maximum light, but there to use when necessary.

Her easel stood there—not the one from her London studio with Amelia and her cat resting upon it, but her old easel, the one from Guy's apartment, and her old draughtsman's board, with a sheet of white sketching paper lying on its top.

On unsteady legs, she walked over to it and looked down. It was the same sketch she had been doing four years ago when her life had fallen apart. She ran her fingertips over the sharp lines of an abstract she had been working on, its image just a blurred memory now, the clean symmetrical lines pulling chords in her creative mind, but not the burning inspiration which had urged her to begin it then.

'Why?' she whispered to the old man watching her in silence from the open door.

He didn't answer straight away, and when eventually she turned to look at him there were tears shining in her blue eyes.

'Why?' she repeated.

'He had everything moved from London to here after this had been completed. It helped him, I think.' His gaze flicked grimly around the sunny room before settling back on Marnie's shock-white face. 'As a kind of therapy, during a time when he was . . .' He paused and grimaced. 'Your continued absence from Oaklands has given it all a maturity. So I suppose this makes it perfect for seeing for the first time.' There was a hint of bitterness in his voice then, and Marnie averted her face, knowing it was probably meant for her.

So, Guy had created this heavenly place for her. The tears grew hotter, burning her eyes as she let them wander over all the other achingly familiar things placed neatly about the room, her emotions in a state of numbing confusion. Shock, surprise, pleasure, pain. And, raking under all of that, suspicion of his motives.

Was this her ivory tower, then? she wondered. The place Guy had always wanted to hide her right away?

'My wife—mine!' He could have been standing right beside her as those fiercely possessive words shot right out of the past to grate fiercely on her senses. He had said them the day they were married, when he took her in his arms for the first time as his wife.

'My son is not guilty of the terrible crime you believe of him, Marnie,' Roberto dropped into the throbbing silence.

She tensed up. 'You don't know what you're talking about,' she dismissed coldly.

Roberto shook his silver head, leaning with the aid of both hands on his elegant walking stick. 'I may be old, my dear,' he murmured drily, 'but I am not senile. And nor am I so surrendered to my infirmity that I am incapable of finding out for myself those things I wish to know.'

Like father, like son, she recognised bitterly. Of course Roberto would have left no stone unturned in his determination to discover why his son's marriage fell apart so dramatically. When Roberto had retired from business, he had done so because he was weary of the constant race for power, not because he was no longer capable of winning the race.

'And,' he went on grimly, 'there were plenty of people present at the fated party willing to relay events as they saw them—not good people,' he conceded to her bitter look. 'But knowledgeable people, none the less.'

'Then you know the truth,' she clipped, and turned away to stare unseeing out of the window, her hair like living flame around her pale face where the sun caught it. 'I would have spared you that, Roberto,' she added bleakly.

'As I said,' he agreed, 'they were not good people. They did not consider an old man's feelings in their eagerness to please his curiosity. But,' he went on, 'on knowing the truth *you* believe, Marnie, my dear, I then have to ask myself why you are allowing yourself to become tied to a man who could so callously use you in that way? Which is why I brought you here,' he added before she could answer. 'I see a recipe for disaster broiling up between you and my son for a second time, and I cannot—will not allow it to happen!'

'Roberto!' she sighed, turning impatiently. 'You can't——'

'My son, Marnie, is using your brother and the delicate condition of his wife to coerce you into marrying him again.' He held up a silencing hand when she went to gainsay it. 'It is no use denying it,' he stated. 'I saw the truth written in your eyes when I quizzed you earlier in my study. You only confirmed my initial suspicions. But, on doing so, I knew I had to act. For, just as I cannot allow Guy to do that to you, nor can I allow you to go on believing a lie cleverly staged for your benefit by wicked and bored people who believe fun can only be gained at the expense of someone else's happiness!'

'But that's all crazy!' she cried, pulling herself together because she suddenly realised that Roberto meant business here. She could see it in the hard flash of his eyes—hints of the ruthless man he used to be before he bestowed all his power on to his son. 'Guy and I are marrying because we find we still love each other!' she insisted, and wondered why the lie did not feel like a lie. 'The past is over! We've come to terms with it and decided to put it all aside! That's all, Roberto!'

'With a four-year-old lie festering between you?' he challenged harshly. 'May I sit down?'

'Oh, goodness! Of course!' Instantly she was all concern when she realised just how long he had been standing on that bad leg. She darted across the room and pulled out a chair for him, then went to help him into it.

'Ah, that's better,' he sighed, then gave his weakened leg an impatient slap. 'You have no idea how much I hate this incapacity!' he complained. 'It makes me want to hit something!'

'You just did,' she said, grinning teasingly at him. 'Your poor leg.'

Roberto grimaced, then smiled himself, and thankfully some of the tension between them faded away—but only for a moment. Roberto caught her wrist as Marnie went to move away again, his grip urgent.

'I brought you here, Marnie, in the hope that seeing this beautiful place my son created for you would soften your heart enough to let you listen to the story I want to tell you. Will you?' He gave the wrist a pleading shake. 'Will you at least listen to what I have to say?'

'Oh, Roberto.' Sighing, she twisted her wrist free. 'Why can't you just leave well alone?'

'Because it just is not good enough!' he grunted. 'Not now. Not when you and Guy are embarking on yet another road to disaster! The truth must come out, Marnie. And the truth is that Guy was so drunk that night you caught him with that woman, he had no idea she was there!'

'My God, Roberto, will you stop it?' she cried, the pain that vision resurrected almost making her sway.

'They saw you enter the party,' he pushed on regardless. 'Fowler and Anthea Cole. They set you up for that tasty little bedroom scene. Fowler hated you because you turned him down when he tried to proposition you. And Anthea hated you because you took her lover away from her! They wanted to see you bleed!'

And they did! Marnie thought as she reeled away from Roberto's fiercely sincere gaze. 'That's enough!' she whispered painfully. 'You are making Guy out to be a blind and gullible fool by saying all of this. And really I don't think he would appreciate it!'

'Too true,' a coldly sardonic voice drawled.

CHAPTER TEN

MARNIE swung round sharply to find Guy standing in the open doorway, the sheer strength of his anger filling the whole aperture.

Roberto muttered something. Then after that there was complete silence, the tension so thick you could almost taste it as Guy flicked his angry gaze from one to the other of them several times before finally settling on Marnie's paste-white features.

'Please leave us, Father,' he sаid, stepping away from the door in a pointed way which had Roberto struggling to his feet and limping towards it.

But he halted when he drew level with his son. 'She has a right to know the truth!' he insisted harshly. 'What you are both doing to each other is wrong! And the truth must come out!'

'I asked you not to interfere in this,' Guy said tightly. 'I did think I had your trust!'

'You have, son, you have,' Roberto sighed wearily. 'What I find sad, though, is that I do not have yours.'

Guy relented a little at his father's crestfallen expression, reaching out a hand to squeeze the old gentleman's shoulder. 'Leave us,' he urged quietly. 'Please.'

'The truth, Guy,' Roberto insisted grimly. 'The only way forward for both of you is through the truth.'

Guy just nodded. And Roberto limped out of the door, leaving them alone and facing each other across the sun-filled room.

Marnie turned her back to Guy, unable to continue looking at him while her mind was running frantically over everything Roberto had said to her. She didn't want to believe him. In fact, she could see what a clever little let-out a story like that could be for someone caught in the situation Guy had been caught in. Yet Guy himself had never tried to excuse his behaviour by feeding her the same story. Or had he? she thought suddenly, her mind filtering back to a scene on the same night she had caught him with Anthea. A scene when she was wild with pain and the bitter humiliation of one who had discovered the very worst about her own husband. When she had flown at him with her nails, and Guy, white-faced and trying desperately to hold her still in front of him, had said something very similar to her. And drunk, she remembered. He had still been half drunk when he had turned up at the apartment that night, could hardly hold himself up straight when he'd lurched into the room.

She heard the quiet closing of the door behind her, then Guy's footsteps sounding on the tiled floor as he crossed the room. Her nerves began to buzz, and she stiffened slightly, not sure what was going to happen next.

She saw, from the corner of her eye, him go to the wide white porcelain sink in one corner and turn on the taps. It was then she realised that he must have come straight from the workshop, because, although he was still wearing the clothes he had travelled down in, he had rid himself of the dark jumper and had rolled back the cuffs of his shirtsleeves to his elbows.

His back was to her, and she turned slightly to watch him take up the bottle of liquid cleaner she used to clean the paint from her fingers, and squeeze some into the palm of his grease-covered hands.

'Well,' he said after a moment, 'what do you think of this place?' He didn't turn, his attention fixed firmly on removing the grease from his long blunt-ended fingers.

'Why?' she asked. 'Why did you build it?'

'As a place you could be happy.' He shrugged, rubbing his hands under the running tap to wash away the dirt. 'I thought,' he went on, reaching for the roll of paper towel and tearing off several squares, 'I thought that if I could create a place beautiful enough for you—somewhere here at Oaklands where you could paint, away from the rest of what goes on here, somewhere you could call entirely your own and even pretend it was miles from anywhere if you wanted to feel that isolated—then maybe you would lose that restless urge you have always possessed to be taking off somewhere alone.'

'An artist's life by necessity is a wandering one, Guy,' she pointed out. 'We need time and space to work to our best potential.'

'Well, here I give you both,' he murmured simply.

'No.' Marnie shook her head. 'You will give me the time and the space to work. You always gave me those things before. But this time you want to take away my right to find inspiration where it takes me. You want to imprison me here!'

'Ah!' He threw away the paper towel, smiling ruefully as he walked over to stand beside her. 'Your precious commissions,' he realised. 'But did you not tell me once, Marnie, that you could paint this valley for a hundred years and never go short of fresh inspiration? Well, now I give you that opportunity.' He waved an expressive hand. 'Paint—paint to your heart's content. The valley awaits your gifted touch.'

'While you do what exactly?' she snapped. 'Go back to London? Coming down here to visit your *contented* wife only when the whim takes you?'

'Do you want me to be here more than the odd weekend?' he challenged.

She didn't answer—found she hadn't got one. Not one she would admit to, anyway. 'Roberto is right,' she murmured after a while. 'We have to both be crazy to be considering returning to that kind of sham again.'

'There was no sham,' he denied, 'just two married people who somehow lost their way. Whether or not we make a better job of our marriage on this second chance will depend entirely on the way we work at it.'

'And working at it, in your book, means me staying tucked away here at Oaklands while you carry on as you've always done in London.'

'I have a business to run.'

'So have I,' she countered, though it had not been quite the point she had been trying to make, her mind still fixed on Anthea as it was.

'Had, Marnie, had,' he corrected. 'Now that you have me to give you everything your heart desires, you no longer need to paint to earn a living, but only to paint because it is what you truly want to paint.'

'On condition I stay within the boundaries of the Oaklands walls, of course.'

'Did I ever make that stipulation?' he challenged. 'I only said you would not be going away for days on end and leaving me as you used to do the last time.'

'And how many days and weeks are you going to spend up in London?' she asked drily.

'None, if you are not with me,' he answered, mocking the surprised look on her face. 'From now on, Marnie, we do everything together. Live together, sleep together, laugh, cry and even fight together, since we seem to like sparring so much.'

A gibe at the way they were sparring now, she supposed. She took in a deep breath and decided to change the subject. 'Roberto tells me you've sent Jamie and Clare off on holiday.'

'He has been busy, hasn't he?' Guy murmured drily. 'Any other little—surprises of mine he has stolen the thunder of?'

She frowned, her thoughts turning back to Roberto's disturbing words. Could there be any truth in them? Could Guy really have been just an innocent victim of his friends' idea of a practical joke?

She took in a deep breath and let it out again on a long, discontented sigh. 'How much of what your father was saying to me did you overhear?' she murmured huskily.

'Most of it.'

'W-was he telling the truth?'

He didn't answer straight away, his attention seemingly fixed on the view beyond the window, then he said quietly, 'You already know the truth. I was unfaithful to you and you caught me out.'

'So, he was lying to me?'

'No,' Guy answered slowly. 'It would not be fair to say he lied exactly—just told it as he prefers to believe it to be.'

'That we were set up,' she nodded. 'That you were an innocent victim of a nasty practical joke and I the blind, gullible fool for believing what my eyes were telling me.'

'Why all this sudden curiosity to know,' he asked, 'when over the last four years you have point-blank refused to so much as think about that damned night?'

'Because—because...' Oh, God. She pushed a hand up to cover her eyes, eyes which were seeing things, things she had refused to attach any importance to before.

Things like the sharp glance Derek Fowler had sent over her shoulder, and the malicious smile on his face when he'd looked back at her. Things like Anthea's equally malicious smile when she had lifted her face out of Guy's throat, her naked limbs wrapped around him; Guy's muffled groan and the blank dazed look in his eyes when he had managed to drag them open, a look that had turned to confusion, then horror, then utter disgust before he'd hoarsely murmured her own name.

Slowly, her face pale with tension, she looked up at him. 'If I ask you now, to explain what happened then, will you tell me?'

'And are you asking?'

Am I? A wave of panic fluttered through her, put there because she had an awful suspicion that, if she said yes, Guy was going to rock the very foundations her life had stood upon over the last four years.

'Yes,' she whispered, dragging her eyes away from him. 'Yes, I am asking.'

There was a moment's silence, while Guy stood beside her with his hands thrust into his trouser pockets. She could sense the indecision in him, the grim reluctance to rake over it all again. Then he sighed, and shifted his posiition, turning to rest his hips on the low window-ledge so he could look directly into her face.

'If I explain what really happened that night,' he said quietly, 'will you in turn explain to me what made you chase up to London looking for me so urgently?'

Marnie lowered her eyes, refusing to answer. 'Your father says we were set up by your friends,' she repeated instead. 'He insists she was there with you without your knowledge. That you were drunk. But you didn't drink!' She sighed, shaking her bright head because her battle with what was the truth and what was lies was beginning to make her head whirl. 'Not in excess, anyway,' she added. She glanced frowningly at him. 'Were you drunk?'

A strange smile touched his lips. 'Out of my mind with it,' he admitted, then grimaced, dropping his gaze and folding his arms across his broad chest to stare grimly at his feet. 'I had been drinking steadily all day. Concerned about you, about the direction our marriage was taking . . .' He looked up, his expression sombre. 'Marnie—our marriage was falling apart at the seams long before the night of that party. We cannot—either of us—blame one isolated incident for its collapse.'

'I know.' Her voice sounded thick. 'But it was the final straw, Guy. One that maybe could have been avoided if...'

'If what?' he asked. 'If I had not taken myself off to Derek's house? If you had not come rushing up to London to find me? If Jamie had not suggested Derek's place to you as a good place to find me? If Anthea had not been such a vindictive little bitch that she was prepared to crucify both of us just to get her revenge on me for replacing her with you?'

'So we *were* set up?'

'Yes.' He sighed heavily. 'I arrived at the party so drunk I could hardly stand...'

'I put him to bed to sleep off the old plonko...' Marnie closed her eyes, quivering on a wave of sickness as she heard Derek Fowler's jeering words echo down the years. Then he had glanced over his shoulder at something or someone on the stairs and that calculating gleam had entered his eyes...

'I did not know a damned thing about anything until I heard you calling to me,' Guy was saying flatly. 'I opened my eyes to see you standing there looking like death. I remember thinking—through the haze of whisky, of course,' he inserted acidly, 'what the hell has happened to make her look like that?' He huffed out a grim laugh, shaking his dark head. 'Then that bitch moved, and I realised she was there, and—well——' he shrugged '—you know the rest.'

Her hand leapt up to cover her trembling mouth, that scene, no matter how false it had been, still having the power to fill her with nausea. 'Oh, God, Guy,' she whispered, not even thinking of questioning his honesty. For some reason she knew it to be the truth.

Four years on, and four years too late, she knew that this was the full destructive truth. 'I'm so sorry...'

'For believing what you were expected to believe?' He lifted his hands emptily in front of him.

'But I should have listened to you, Guy!' she choked out, feeling wretched in her own guilt. 'I could have at least given you the chance to explain!'

'Explain what?' he asked. 'That what you saw with your own eyes was an illusion?' He shook his dark head. 'I tell you this, Marnie—if the roles had been reversed between you and me, I would not have listened. I would not have believed.'

'Is that supposed to make me feel better?' she demanded shrilly. 'To know that for the last four years I've been punishing you for something you didn't even do!'

'I was not aware that we were discussing this with the aim of making you feel better,' he mocked drily. 'I thought we were supposed to be simply sharing the truth!'

'A truth you should have made me listen to long ago!' she cried. 'A truth you *would* have made me listen to if it had been at all important to you that I hear it!'

'Are you trying to imply that I did not care?' he demanded incredulously. 'After the way I have let you wipe your feet on my feelings for the last four years, are you actually daring to——?'

'God, no,' she sighed, accepting that his burst of anger was well deserved. She had been at it again—no sooner believing him to be the innocent party in a game that had ripped her world apart than she was accusing him of another unjustified sin.

In fact, she realised starkly, it seemed that it was Guy who should be doing the accusing, and she who should be begging forgiveness.

Forgiveness for a lot of things. Some of them that he—thankfully—knew nothing about! And never would, she vowed grimly. Never.

So? she wondered dully, seeing no use in a marriage between them now. Not unless Guy was planning to take revenge on her for the four years. She glanced at him sitting there in profile to her, deep in his own private brooding.

He always did brood magnificently, she noted when her heart picked up a few beats as she studied him. But then, she wryly extended on that thought, he tended to do everything magnificently. Shout, laugh, run, dance, sing, drive his fast cars—make love!

The sun was gleaming on the top of his head, adding depth to the sleek blue-blackness of his hair. His skin—born to have the sun caress it, glowing rich and sexy.

He was a man of wildly exciting contrasts. Far, far too much for her to deal with five years ago. Did she have any hope of dealing with him any better now? She didn't think so. Guy was one of those rare people who belonged exclusively to himself. What bit he did give out of himself was maybe enough for other women, but not for her. Wasn't that the main reason why she had fought against his power when they had first met—because she had wanted more from him than she'd known he would ever want to give?

'Why did you ever marry me at all, Guy?' she asked impulsively. 'I mean, it was obvious to everyone, including all your friends, that I was way out of my depth with you. So what made you marry someone like me?'

'Because I could not help myself, I suppose.' He grimaced. 'It was either marry you or lock you away so no other man could get you. I wanted your innocence, Marnie,' he taunted cruelly. 'All of it. Every last exquisite bit of it. So I flattered you with my lethal charm, and impressed you with my dynamic sex appeal!'

'Stop it,' she snapped, frowning because she suspected his mockery was aimed entirely at himself.

'Seduced and bullied you,' he continued regardless, 'then waited for the magic I had so carefully woven around you to wear off, and that delightful hero-worship you repaid me with to——'

'I never did hero-worship you!' she exclaimed, appalled by the very idea.

'Did you not?' He lifted a challenging brow at her. 'Then why did you marry me, Marnie?' he threw back silkily.

She looked away, refusing to answer. What was the use? She should have told him she loved him five years ago when their marriage still had a chance. It was too late now—much, much too late.

'No answer?' He laughed softly. 'So instead give me an answer to the question I asked you earlier, if you will. Why did you come chasing up to London that fated night?' He waited for some time in the deadly silence which followed, then laughed softly again. 'No answer yet again,' he mocked. 'It seems to me, Marnie, that all the secrets between us have not yet been fully aired. Still,' he dismissed, coming to his feet, 'we have time for all of that. Plenty of time now to learn about each other—perhaps better than we managed the first time we married.'

'You can't seriously still be considering marrying me after what's come out today!' she cried, staring at him in horror.

'But Marnie,' he drawled sardonically, 'you seem to forget. I knew it all before today.'

'And now I know!' she cried. 'Guy—I wronged you! It has to change things!'

'What has changed other than that you now know I am gullible enough to allow myself to become so drunk I did not know what I was doing—or who I was doing it with? Does knowing I was in no fit state to know what was going on condone that kind of behaviour?' he demanded. 'Is it OK to find me in bed with another woman so long as you can blame it on the evil drink?'

'No,' she whispered. 'But——' That wasn't how it happened, she was going to say, but he cut her short.

'Then I am guilty as always charged,' he snapped. 'And that is all that needs to be said on the subject.' He turned away. 'Come on,' he said flatly. 'Dinner will be ready soon and I haven't even shown you to your room.'

'But Guy!' she appealed in exasperation. 'We can't just——'

'Enough!' He turned suddenly, and in one lurching stride was back in front of her. The flash of blazing anger burning in his eyes was the only warning she got before he grabbed her and pulled her hard against him.

What followed was a forceful and angry method of silencing her. By the time he let her go again she was trembling so badly she could barely stand up.

'That is all that matters now, Marnie,' he said harshly. 'You still want me physically. And God knows I still want you! So, we remarry in two days' time——'

'Two days?' she choked. 'But——'

'No buts,' he inserted. 'We made a bargain. I have stuck to my part in it and you will stick to yours. And you will do it,' he warned threateningly, 'with a smile on your face that will convince my father that nothing on this earth can part us a second time!' He reached for her chin, holding it between finger and thumb with just enough pressure to let her know he could hurt her if he wished to. 'Got that?'

Licking her throbbing lips, she nodded uncertainly.

'Right,' he said. 'Then let's go.' He turned his back on her, walking arrogantly to the door and throwing it open. She followed him wearily, wondering what the hell she was following him into.

They were married as decreed, two days later, by the local registrar, followed by having their union blessed by a Catholic priest whose liberal thinking—plus a generous donation to his church roof fund—allowed him to forget the fact that they had once been married and divorced.

'A life sentence this time, Marnie,' Guy murmured with grim satisfaction as they drove back to the house. 'Do you think you can stand it?'

He was being sarcastic because he was well aware that she had only just controlled the urge to run and keep on running before her actual 'sentencing' became official.

Whatever Guy had told his father when they had locked themselves away in Roberto's study the other night she had no idea, but he had clearly allayed his father's fears, because Roberto had looked as pleased as punch ever since! Aided and abetted by Guy, of course, who missed no opportunity to force Marnie into confirming their undying love for each other in front of the old man.

Roberto kissed her on both cheeks then formally welcomed her back into the family. 'Not,' he adjoined, 'that we ever considered you anything else. Now what you both need is half a dozen pairs of tiny feet running about the place,' he grinned. 'That is the surest way of giving neither of you any time to think of falling out again!'

She felt herself go pale. The only thing stopping her from losing her balance on suddenly shaky legs was Guy's arm fixed like a vice around her waist.

'When we are ready, Papa, and not before,' he threw back lightly. 'So take that twinkle of anticipation out of your eyes for now.'

'I'm going to the studio,' she informed Guy tensely as soon as his father disappeared into his study.

'Running away again?' he mocked.

'Where to?' she snapped back. 'You know as well as I do that there is nowhere left for me to run to. You've closed down all escape routes,' she reminded him. 'So even my brother isn't mine any more.'

'You have me,' he said quietly. 'Think about it, Marnie. When have you not had me to run to since the day we met?'

'The day I lost——' She had her lips snapped shut just in time, eyes closing out the sudden anguish in her eyes. 'Do you really mind if I go to the studio for an hour or two?' she pleaded anxiously.

'Why?' he murmured a trifle cynically. 'Will it make a difference if I say I do mind?'

'Of course it will make a difference!' She sighed, unable to hold back the note of frustration in her voice. 'But...'

'You are riddled with bridal nerves,' he suggested, so poker-faced she could have hit him.

'Please, Guy!' she was driven to plead with him. If it wasn't bad enough that he was wearing the most exquisite black suit, made of pure silk, that did the most disturbing things to his muscle-packed frame, then he had to taunt her with the lazy mockery of his liquid brown eyes, offering promises with them that turned her insides to jelly. 'Let me go! Just while I get used to——'

'Being married again,' he inserted for her. And, as if tuned in to what was really bothering her, he let his own eyes run slowly over the simple cream silk suit dress she was wearing beneath its matching bolero jacket. A dress with a heart-shaped boned bodice that stayed up of its own volition and showed more than enough of her shadowed cleavage. She had taken her hair away from her face with two creamy combs, then left it to tumble in a riot of loose curls down her back. He took it all in: the dress, the cleavage, the hairstyle and the anxious face it flattered so nicely; then he let his eyes come firmly on to hers.

'I'm sorry, Marnie,' he said quietly. 'But today is special, and I insist we spend it together.'

So by the time the 'day' grew to its inevitable conclusion Marnie was so uptight about what came next that even a long soak in a hot bath could not ease the tension from her aching body.

It took Guy to do that. With his usual devastating force.

He was standing in the shadows of the deep bay window when she eventually came out of the adjoining bathroom. The curtains had not yet been drawn, and Guy seemed engrossed in whatever he could see beyond the bedroom window. A bedroom lit by the muted glow from one small light bulb hidden beneath the pale gold shade of the bedside lamp. A bedroom they had shared before.

A bedroom they were about to share again.

Her stomach knotted, that awful tension centering itself in one vulnerable spot.

So this was it, she told herself nervously. Pay-up time.

Did she have it in her to just give herself to him as though the wedding-ring now gleaming on her finger automatically made it right?

He looked oddly remote standing there so deeply lost in his own thoughts that he wasn't even aware of her presence. A big, lean man dressed in nothing more than his usual black silk robe. A man whose natural dark colouring seemed to reflect the mood surrounding him tonight, more so while he stood as deep in the shadows as he did.

She chewed down uncertainly on her bottom lip, not quite knowing what she should do next.

Either climb in the bed and think of England, Marnie, she mocked herself acidly, or show a little grace in defeat and go and stand beside him.

She chose the latter, but it took all the courage she had left in her to force her bare feet to walk silently across the thick wool carpet until she reached his side.

'It—it's a beautiful night,' she observed, then could have bitten off her tongue for coming out with such a silly opening remark as that.

Her face muscles clenched, waiting for him to make some mockingly sarcastic remark in return. But he didn't. Didn't say anything for a while, and the tension in her increased, making her tremble a little, wishing herself a million miles away. Wishing she'd had the sense to run and keep on running the moment Jamie had walked into her flat with his latest problem.

'They forecast rain for later,' Guy answered suddenly, making her jump. Her reaction brought his hooded gaze on her. 'You look beautiful,' he murmured, a dry twist of a smile spoiling the compliment. 'Quite the perfect sacrifice, in fact.'

Unexpected tears began to fill her eyes so she had to avert her face until she had blinked them firmly away, finding this role reversal from being the wronged to the wrongdoer very difficult to cope with. And his sarcasm only managed to make her feel more tense, more miserable.

She could feel his eyes still on her, and the familiar tingling sensation started seeping its way throughout her system, beginning in that ball of tension in her stomach then slowly spreading out until it had encompassed every part of her, from the very roots of her softly falling hair to the tips of her fingers and toes.

Then suddenly he reached for her, his two hands spanning her waist to lift her off the ground before settling her back on her feet directly in front of him.

She glanced up, startled and wary, but Guy's attention was on her hair, his fingers coming up to thread absently through the long, loose tresses, then down to her shoulders where only the flimsy bootlace straps of her pale pink nightgown stopped the fine silk from slithering to her feet. He ran light fingertips over her skin, and down her arms, raising goose-bumps where he touched.

'Do you think,' he murmured in a deep quiet voice that revealed an odd touch of bleakness, 'that as the years go by the gap in our ages will narrow?' He took up her hands and held them loosely in his own, studying them with his dark lashes lowered over his eyes. 'You look very young tonight, Marnie,' he added huskily. 'As young as the first time we stood together on a night like this. Do I, by contrast, look as old to you?'

Old? she thought, almost smiling at the idea. Guy was not and never would be 'old'. She had never understood this one small chink in an otherwise impregnable armour of self-confidence.

Her blue eyes drifted across the lean, sleek lines of his face with the detailed intensity of a trained artist. Guy was the most beautiful man she had ever seen. There wasn't a single thing about his physical appearance she would want to change.

How could someone like him seem to need reassurance from someone like her? She didn't understand it—never had before.

'No,' she answered him at last. That was all. Just that one simple word that to her said it all—and sent some unknown emotions flashing across his face.

He lifted his eyes and let them clash with hers; dark and burning, telling her without words what he was thinking, feeling—wanting. She shuddered, not sure she could answer the look, and had to look down and away.

'If I never made you feel loved in my arms before, Marnie,' he muttered thickly, 'then I promise you that tonight you will feel it right through to your very soul!'

He caught her mouth, not harshly, as his tone had been, but with a kiss so achingly gentle that she found herself responding almost without realising it.

He still held her hands, and he lifted them around his neck. The action arched her body closer to his, and he spanned her slender waist, holding her close while slowly—oh, so slowly—deepening the kiss into something beyond sweetness.

Her lips parted easily, her tongue waiting to tangle sensually with his. He breathed deeply on a sigh. So did she, and it seemed to herald an end to the final threads of inner resistance she had been trying to cling on to. She wanted this. Why should she pretend otherwise when this was what she had been pining for for days now—since that wild scene at his apartment the morning after they'd arrived there?

And perhaps even before that, a small voice suggested. Perhaps you've been pining for this for years.

Her hands moved to find the collar of his robe, fingers creeping beneath it, sliding against his warm skin and urging the robe away from his shoulders at the same time. She revelled in the heated silk of his smooth shoulders, in the muscled tension in his upper arms, the robe sliding slowly away until she had exposed the full beauty of his hair-covered chest.

Guy gave a shudder of pleasure as she dragged her mouth from his to capture a male nipple instead, sucking on it, biting at it in a way that made his chest expand on a pleasurable gasp, and her fingers moved to untie the robe, setting his whole body free, giving her access to his lean waist, his tight buttocks and long hair-roughened thighs.

Her nightgown rippled down her body to land in a silken pool of pink ice at her feet. His hands were on her body, stroking with slow feather-light caresses that tempted each nerve-end to come to the surface of her skin so her pleasure was heightened, making her groan and arch and sway with his touch.

'Marnie . . .' he murmured when she ran her fingers along his highly sensitive groin, catching her roving hand tightly in his own. 'Don't,' he whispered. 'My control is not that good.'

She found his mouth again, swamping out the need for words with a kiss that was so sensual, it fired his blood. And he arched her slender body so it bent like a supple wand against the pulsing rock of his.

And they began to move across the dimly lit room in a kind of primeval love dance that brought them to the bed. When he had eased her down on the pale peach cover he took great care to smooth her long hair out behind her, his expression intent, as though he was acting out some private fantasy of his own.

Marnie lay very still, watching him through dark unguarded eyes. When he caught her gaze he smiled, a soft kind of smile that was so infinitely gentle that it touched something achingly beautiful inside her, and she smiled back, reaching up to pull him down on her.

He went, covering her naked body with his own as though understanding her need at that moment to feel again his total mastery over her in the full weight of his body pressing down on hers.

Their mouths joined and remained joined, even as their caresses became more heated, more intimate. Need began to build like a coiled spring inside both of them, building and building until on a sob she spread her legs and wound them invitingly around him.

It was all the prompting he needed. He entered her on a single swift, sure thrust, then lay heavily against her, his heart, like her own, thundering out of control, mouths still locked while he battled to maintain some control over himself.

She had closed around him like a silken sheath, taking in and holding the pulsing force of him deep, deep inside her.

Then, 'Love me,' she whispered breathlessly.

'I've always loved you, Marnie,' he murmured thickly back. 'How could you ever believe otherwise?'

'No!' she whimpered, shaking her head because she didn't want to hear those words, didn't want to have to think about them, dissect them, understand the devastating import of what they meant.

'Oh, yes, angel,' he sighed out caressingly. 'Yes.'

He moved then, and suddenly words didn't matter. Their bodies were so in tune that they climbed together in a rhapsody of deep, slow body movements, and when the climax did come it hit her with a sudden racing of the pulses, and that wonderful high tensile floating of the senses held her hovering for endless moments of incredible beauty before she was released, pulling Guy with her into the storm awaiting them, ripples becoming waves, and waves a riptide of pure sensation that carried them on and on before finally, inevitably letting them swim lazily into quieter waters.

They lay spent for a long time before either of them felt willing to move. And then only Guy seemed to find the strength to do it, sliding away from her then reaching to flip back the covers before lifting her gently beneath them and joining her there.

He took her back into his arms, and Marnie lay wrapped in the wonderful afterglow of a beautiful experience, her mind still drifting somewhere high above the clouds, limbs heavy, body replete, senses content to settle back into a languid calm while she listened to the comforting throb of his heartbeat beneath her cheek.

Guy moved again, scooping up the thick curtain of her hair and giving it one gentle twist around his fist—as he always used to do—just before he set it on the pillow behind her.

Then he settled his cheek lightly on top of her head, brushed his lips against her hair and said quietly, 'Tell me about the child we made and lost, Marnie,' and succeeded in exploding her contented world into a million broken pieces.

CHAPTER ELEVEN

MARNIE came awake the next morning to find herself alone. And only the imprint on the pillow beside her said that Guy had ever been there.

But he had been, she remembered dully. Carefully, steadily—ruthlessly stripping her of every last layer of protection she had grown around herself over the years until all that was left was the raw and tortured woman he found beneath.

So, now he knew everything. She had told him the lot, dumping it all on his lap with a bitter malice which showed how thoroughly he had deranged her with his cruel shock-tactics.

And if she had locked it all away inside her because it was the only way to deal with the pain of it all, then the opening up of that terrible door had inflicted double the pain, double the anger and double the guilt for what she saw as her own unforgivable selfishness in running away as she had, giving no thought to the fragile life growing inside her.

To be fair to Guy, when it had all come pouring out, he had held on to her tightly, refusing to let go even when she fought him like a wildcat in an effort to break free.

Oh, he had held her close, given her his strength and his comfort throughout the whole ordeal. But he had not been satisfied until he had wrenched every last detail from her.

'You should have told me all this a long time ago!' he had censured angrily when her sobs had threatened to tear her apart inside. 'Look how it hurts for its four years' festering. See what you do to yourself now.'

'How did you find out?' she asked when she had enough control over herself to wonder at his uncanny knowledge. She had told no one about her poor baby. No one. Not even Clare, when she'd gone through a similar tragedy.

'Let's just leave it that I did know,' he said grimly. 'For now it is all out in the open, Marnie, it should be let go. God knows, we've both suffered enough over it—more than enough.'

For some reason, the dull throb in his voice set her crying all over again. He drew her closer, and it was in his arms that she fell asleep—only to wake up to find him gone.

And she didn't dare wonder what that had to mean.

It was then she heard it—the distinctive growl of a powerful engine revving in the distance. She climbed out of bed and, grabbing the loose end of the sheet, wrapped it around her naked body and moved over to the window to wait, knowing that the sound meant that Guy was already down at the track and preparing to take out one of his cars.

It must have rained in the night, she noticed. The air had a fresh, damp smell about it, the lawns below her sparkling in the weak morning sun. She could see the stream babbling more fiercely down towards the lake. And over to the west, just beyond the valley itself, she could see more clouds gathering, thick and dark, promising yet more rain soon.

But the sun still shone on Oaklands, and Roberto's roses seemed happy enough to lift their heads and open their petals, so maybe the storm was not coming this way——

She heard it then, the sudden change in motor noise, followed quickly by a throaty roar which said Guy had put the car in gear and was speeding smoothly out of the pit lane.

She had often stood here like this waiting for him to go flashing by in some sleek growling monster at awe-inspiring speed. And she closed her eyes now, so she could watch with her mind's eye him shoot out of the pit lane on to the track itself, each small cut in engine sound denoting a split-second change in gear.

He was already in top gear by the time he hit the track, accelerating away down the main straight on a roar which set her pulses racing along with it. In a second or two he would reach the first sharp curve which sent the track into a tricky S-bend. She heard the distinctive sound as he changed down, the throaty noise as he throttled back followed by the frightening surge of power that said he was out of the bend and accelerating towards the bridge which would take him over the stream then on around the lake until he hit the straight directly in front of the house, coming into her view just as he cleared the water.

Her breath caught in anticipation, eyes wide with a mixture of excitement and fear, for when he hit the length of road in front of her it meant he would have whichever car it was he had decided to take out travelling at its maximum speed.

But it was only when she saw the flash of blue and white as he came into view that she realised he wasn't driving one of the beautiful museum pieces, but the Frabosa Formula One.

The updated and daunting car was similar to the one he had won his world championships in, but had since moved on a pace in its development to become one of the best cars on the circuit this decade. Guy had decided to include this one in his collection as a testimony to his own success.

And it was the car she hated the most, for its gruesome power, for its flimsy build, and for its total lack of respect for anything human. And because Guy only ever drove that awful car when he was in the blackest of moods.

But what had her heart thudding heavily in her breast as she watched him fly past was the knowledge that he was driving that thing because of what she had told him last night. She was sure of it, just as she was suddenly sickeningly sure that he had taken the blame for their lost child entirely on himself.

With her eyes tightly closed, and lips drawn tight across her teeth, her ears took up her whole concentration, listening for and interpreting each minute sound the engine made for signs of malfunction. Or, worse—any bad timing on the driver's part. You didn't spend twelve months of your life around men like Guy without learning quickly the sounds which mattered.

He should be changing gear—now!

He did. Marnie wilted gratefully. The timing was that crucial. For, after the straight in front of the house, he had to negotiate the chicane, a cleverly constructed piece of engineering which also took him back across the stream again, through a series of tricky bends then back towards the main section in front of the pits.

She followed each sound all the way around, knowing to within a metre just where the car should be.

By the time he hit the pits straight he would really be opening up the throttle, his tyres warmed and ready to respond to his lightest command. It would be the second or maybe the third circuit before he was really flying. And then the crew would be out with their stop-watches, clocking his track time, just as they would do in a real race.

Trembling, she spun away from the window and made for the dressing-room, dragging on a pair of jeans and a sweatshirt without bothering with underwear, determined to be back at the window by the time he came past again.

She just made it, breathing fast. He roared past at full throttle, a mere blur on her vision. And she closed her eyes on a silent prayer that he would judge the first bend correctly.

He did. She held her breath. The chicane next. Through—tyres prostesting when he must have touched one of the concrete kerbs on a slight error of judgement.

Don't do it again! she scolded him silently as he began negotiating the series of bends. Then the smooth roar as he reached full speed past the pits. She waited for him to reach the S-bend, hating his need to test himself in such a way. Hating even more his reason for doing it.

Marnie watched him go by her a third time, and knew with a sinking heart that he had to be driving that car with the turbo charger full on, because she had never seen it go so fast! She almost dropped to the floor with relief when he got safely around the next bend, then the chicane—it was like having her own personal scaled-down model running around her head, she could be that accurate on where he was at any moment.

The straight in front of the pits again, and the roar as he boosted the turbo, the sound seeming to fill the whole valley. Then the S-bend——

She waited breathlessly for the familiar protest from the engine as he throttled back sharply—and certainly the change-down did occur, but the immediate uplift of power never followed it. Instead there was the tooth-grating sound of squealing brakes and screaming tyres followed all too quickly by nothing.

Absolute silence.

For a full five seconds Marnie didn't move a muscle, the echo of those screaming tyres consuming her every sense, while she used those few precious seconds to accept what had happened.

Then she was running, barefoot, out of the bedroom, along the landing and down the stairs. Hair streaming out behind her, face pure white, she ran across the hall, past Roberto without stopping, even though some sane portion of her mind told her that he too must have heard the crash and understood its frightening possibilities. But she was too wrapped up in her own terror to stop, running out of the door and around the side of the house, racing across neatly shorn lawns, slipping on the wet grass as she went, knowing exactly where she was making for, exactly at what spot Guy had spun the car.

She saw the plume of thick black smoke curling up into the sky just as she reached the thick hedge which separated the track from the house, and she stopped, taking this next horror with a choking whimper before she was off and running again, forcing herself through the hedge without a care to the scratches it issued to her arms and face. Careless of everything but the one thought that was going around and around in her head.

Guy was dead, and she had not told him she loved him.

She saw the emergency van at the scene as she rounded a curve in the track. The red van was parked at an angle, its doors all swinging open. The blue and white car was not far away, lost to a blaze of fire and smoke while the men fought to contain the flames. White clouds of foam were emitting from their hand-held extinguishers, fluffy particles of the stuff floating in the air all around them.

Dismay took her legs from under her, sending her tumbling to the ground, her choked cry of horror splitting the air around her. Then she struggled up again, pushing her hair out of her face, terrified of going on yet drawn by some morbid desire to see, witness the worst for herself.

It was as she neared the emergency van that she saw him. He was standing by one of the open doors, his left hand holding his right shoulder, his attention fixed on the tangled mess which was all that was left of the car.

For some reason, seeing him just standing there as large as life, silver flame-proofed suit hardly marked, protective helmet still firmly on his head, Marnie lost touch with reality, and on a surge of white hot fury she launched herself at him.

'You crazy, stupid man!' she yelled, the grinding force of her voice bringing his head sharply around to see her running furiously towards him.

'Marnie...' He put out his left hand in a calming gesture. 'It's all right. I am not——'

But she wasn't listening. Rage consumed her. And on a cry that came out like an animal howl she threw herself at him, hitting out with her fists, tears pouring down her cheeks, eyes almost blind with shock and anger.

Guy tried to field her blows by catching her fists, but she was too quick and he was still feeling dazed from the crash. And she caught him on his right shoulder, making him wince, and draw back instinctively.

Then someone was catching her from behind. And a different voice tried bringing the tirade to a halt. 'Mrs Frabosa!' it said sternly. 'The man is injured; you can't——'

'Let go of her,' Guy rasped. Marnie was sobbing by now, great big racking sobs that by far outstripped the ones she had sobbed the night before. 'Let go of her, Tom.'

'But she——'

'Let go.'

The man set her free and stood back, but ready, despite what his employer said, to catch her if she made another attack on Guy.

But she had already hit herself out, the anger replaced with a deep inner ache that sent her crumbling to her knees on the wet ground in front of them.

She looked pathetic, jeans scuffed, bare feet all muddied, hair a tangled mess around her face and shoulders, and hands shaking so violently that she had to clutch them together on her lap to keep them still.

Guy muttered something beneath his breath, trying to unclip the strap holding his helmet in place.

'Dammit, Tom!' he rasped. 'Do this for me, will you?'

He stood impatiently while Tom struggled with the strap, both men more concerned with the state Marnie had got herself into than the car or Guy's injuries now.

'Shock,' Tom muttered. 'She must have thought——'

'I know exactly what she thought,' Guy cut in grimly.

The helmet came off, followed by the white flame-proof snood he always wore beneath. 'Get back to the car,' he said to Tom, thrusting both items at him, then dropped down on his knees in front of Marnie, shielding her from the sympathetic glances she was receiving from the rest of the team, but not attempting to touch her while he waited once again for her to cry herself out.

After a while, he sighed heavily and glanced at the burned-out remains of the car, steaming passively now. The first spot of rain hit his cheek, and even as he went to wipe it away the deluge came, drenching them all in seconds.

'If the fire is out, then get back to the house and let my father know I am OK,' he told the crew.

They went quickly, glad to get out of the rain but curious as to why Guy was just kneeling there in front of his wife, doing nothing in the way of either trying to comfort her or protecting them both from the deluge.

They drove away in the red van. Guy watched them go, his eyes grim and bleak. Then he turned his attention back to Marnie, and, still without attempting to touch her, began to talk, quietly, levelly, with little to no emotion sounding in his tone, and she went silent as she knelt there in front of him, listening, with her heart locked in her aching throat.

'You know,' he began, 'the first time I saw you, here in the yard behind the house, I thought to myself, My God, this is it. The one I have been waiting for for so many years! I wanted to grab hold of you there and then and never let you go. But even as I stood there just drinking you in I could also see that you were about the most innocent creature I had ever laid eyes on. I knew, also, that it would be wrong of me to follow my greedy instincts, though. I was too old for you—oh, not only in years,' he sighed out heavily, 'but in experience. In life! I had done too much, seen too much, and, God help me, *been* too much to be even daring to consider contaminating you with it all. And you possessed special self-protective instincts, too. Instincts that warned you to have nothing to do with a cynical old devil like me. You disapproved of me, Marnie, from the moment our eyes clashed.'

'I didn't disapprove of you,' she denied, the rain pouring on to the top of her bowed head and running down the long pelt of her hair.

Even with her face averted, she knew he smiled. 'You did, Marnie,' he insisted. 'Disapproved of everything about me. My so-called friends. My arrogance. My rather notorious reputation—even my practised methods of seduction! The only glimmer of hope you ever allowed me then was the fact that you could not stop yourself responding to me despite the disapproval! And it was that—need you developed for my physical touch that I exploited ruthlessly to get you to marry me,' he admitted, 'then spent the next year trying to live up to the illusion I had created that it was just your body I coveted. When all the time, Marnie——' his hand came up to lightly touch her cheek '—what I coveted deeply was your love.'

'Oh, Guy,' Marnie sighed. 'How can such an intelligent man be so stupid?'

'Stupid just about says it,' he agreed. 'I knew you were pregnant with our child, Marnie,' he told her, swallowing down on the sudden lump which had formed in his throat. Unable to look at her, he glanced over the track to where the house stood shrouded by the pounding rain. 'Even before you came looking for me that night, I knew.'

'But you couldn't have!' she cried. 'I didn't even know myself!'

'But I did not know that.' He faced her grimly. 'I came back from my business trip to find you standing there looking so wan and frail that it just—hit me—and I knew you were pregnant.' He shrugged helplessly. 'It was logical to assume that you must know also. But you never said a word about it to me, and you looked so unhappy, as if a child between us was the last thing on earth you wanted, and I was hurt, enough to want to hurt you in return, so I threw some nasty little remark at you about the mess you looked, and turned round and walked out again!'

'And didn't come back again that night,' she inserted painfully.

'I sat in my car, in the basement car park,' he confessed, smiling bleakly at her look of surprise. 'Sat there all night just thinking, feeling rotten for speaking to you like that, and seething with my own hurt because you could not bring yourself to even tell me we had made a child! I came back into the apartment the next morning——'

'Looking as if you'd just crawled out of someone's bed to come straight home.'

He nodded, his expression rueful. 'I know exactly how I must have looked to you,' he acknowledged. 'So we started rowing again, and, in the end—through sheer desperation more than anything else because you were actually voicing the idea of leaving me by then—I packed you off down here. Told you brutally to choose between me and your precious work. Smiled and waved arrogantly at you and drove away. Back to London and to blessed relief in a whisky bottle.'

'Not expecting me to come chasing up to London when I eventually realised I was pregnant, wanting only to share the news with you.'

'But instead you found me with another woman.' He lifted his pained eyes to hers. 'That was the night I came to realise just how much you loved me,' he said roughly. 'And just how much I had lost.'

'But Guy,' Marnie frowned, 'if you never knew before how much I loved you, then how——?'

'You were destroyed, Marnie,' he said. 'I destroyed you that night you found me in bed with Anthea. And it does not matter whether I was innocent or not, or whether I was too drunk to know anything about it or not. The simple fact of the matter was that I had been so busy hiding my own love from you that I had not even noticed you were loving me too! And when you flew at me when I got home that night you did not do it in anger, but with all the pain and anguish of one who saw their hopes and dreams lying dead and bloodied at their feet. Only a heart bleeds like that, Marnie. I know because my own heart bled along with yours.'

'Oh, Guy,' Marnie whispered unhappily. 'Of course it matters! There's a whole world of difference between seeing your husband in bed with another woman because it's where he prefers to be, and seeing your husband in bed with another woman because his awful friends thought it a great way of having some fun with his stupid young wife while he was too drunk to do anything about it!'

'But how did I explain that to you?' he challenged her logic. 'How does a man who has taken great care to make you believe that he only wants you for your delicious body—and was even guilty of threatening to take another woman to his bed when the one he wanted was making herself unavailable to him—how does a man like that defend himself in that kind of damning situation? How could you allow yourself to believe other than what you saw? I had no leg to stand on,' he sighed, 'and I knew, as I watched your love for me turn to hatred in front of my very eyes, that I deserved every last thing I was going to get from you. Though, God, Marnie,' he ground out, 'those six months you disappeared out of sight will always go down as the worst time of my life!

'Then you came back,' he went on hoarsely. 'And the moment I saw your slender figure and that awful lifeless expression in your eyes I knew that the child was gone. And that I was to blame.' He cleared his thickened throat. 'I knew then that I was way beyond forgiveness.'

'So all along,' Marnie concluded, 'when you've talked of penances, you've meant because you blamed yourself because I lost our baby, and not because of Anthea and what I believed you had done.'

He nodded grimly. 'If I had loved you better, Marnie, then——'

'I had a fall, Guy!' she inserted shrilly. 'Neither you nor I could be to blame for that! I fell. I told you last night. I stumbled and fell down some steps. A tragic accident. No one's fault.'

'My fault,' he insisted. 'You are not a careless creature, Marnie. If I had taken better care of you, loved you so openly that you could never have doubted me in any situation you caught me in, then you would not have run away from me. And you would not have become so wrapped up in your misery as to allow yourself to fall!'

'So,' she said, 'because you decided to take the whole guilt of it on to yourself, you then decided the best thing you could do for both of us was jump into that—rotten car and drive it at speeds guaranteed to kill!'

'No.' Reaching out, he took hold of her, dragging her into his arms. 'Never,' he denied. 'I have no intention of ever leaving you again. Be clear on that. But you know my black devils, Marnie. When they drive me I have to answer to them. And behind the wheel of a car I am as cool as a cucumber, clear-headed and clear-eyed. A tyre blew, that's why I spun off the track,' he explained. 'It had nothing to do with my bad driving, or the speed I was travelling at. Or even my trying my best to die for love of you!' he mocked. 'It was just the simple result of a faulty tyre. Nothing else.'

She looked dubiously over at the wrecked car. 'But you could have killed yourself.'

'Impossible,' he said with more his usual arrogance. 'I am too good a driver. Even at speeds of one hundred and fifty miles an hour these cars can be controlled on three wheels. They are built for safety, no matter how flimsy they look.'

'They set on fire at the drop of a hat, too,' she pointed out.

'Which is why I wear all this protective gear, so I can still climb out relatively unscathed.'

It was only then that they both seemed to become aware of the rain pouring relentlessly down on their heads. Of the puddle they were kneeling in. Of their dripping heads and muddy clothes, and their cold, wet faces.

'You look a mess,' Marnie observed frankly. 'And you've hurt yourself—here.' She touched a wet fingertip to his cheek where a bruise was already beginning to swell.

'And you have scratches all over your arms and face.' Guy returned the tender gesture by touching his fingers to the thin red scratch-marks on her cheeks. 'How did they happen?'

'Coming to rescue you,' she told him, blue eyes twinkling ruefully. 'I had to fight my way through a hedge and it fought back—kiss it better?' she murmured huskily.

Guy looked deeply into her love-darkened eyes, then slowly placed a kiss on each red mark. 'Anywhere else?' he enquired as he drew away.

'Oh, all over, I think,' she sighed, the feather-like feel of his mouth leaving her skin tingling with pleasure. 'What about you?' she then asked in sudden concern. 'Did you hurt yourself anywhere else other than that bruise on your eye?'

'Oh, all over, I think,' he mimicked hopefully.

'Seriously?' she demanded.

'Seriously,' he mocked. 'I bashed my shoulder a bit when the car lurched off the track, then received some other more—er—delicate injuries when a wild woman came at me from nowhere and began beating me up!'

'Oh.' She pouted, remembering her mad attack. 'I was angry with you.'

'I did notice,' he drawled.

'Well,' she defended herself, 'I expected to find you dead, at least! And there you were standing there looking as fit as a blooming fiddle!'

'Is there something worse than death?' he enquired curiously.

'Yes,' Marnie answered, her expression suddenly very serious. 'A lifetime of never knowing how much I love you, Guy.'

'Come here,' he muttered, pulling her against him and wrapping her tightly in his arms. 'You are all I have ever wanted in my life from the moment you entered it, Marnie.'

'Then let's go home, Guy,' she whispered. 'I want to hold you close in that big warm bed I woke up feeling so alone in this morning.'

'Bed?' His mood brightened, his manner with it. 'That has to be a better option than a puddle any day,' he agreed, pulling her to her feet as he got up himself. 'A long hot bath sounds good, too,' he added leeringly.

'A bath for two?' Marnie suggested, tucking her arm around his waist while he hugged her by her shoulders. She lifted her wet face up to him and let her eyes twinkle with promises.

Guy growled something and began to run, dashing with her through the rain towards the house.

'I could paint you looking like this, all wet and sexily tousled,' Marnie told him a few minutes later when they were safely locked behind their bedroom door.

'Not today, you couldn't,' Guy said firmly. 'Today I have other of your—talents to call upon. Mainly making this man you married happy.'

'Be happy, Guy,' she said softly and reached up on tiptoe to brush his lips with hers.

'I will be,' he said, pulling her close again, 'so long as you never leave me again.'

'Never,' she promised. 'You're stuck with me for life.'

INDULGE A LITTLE 6947 SWEEPSTAKES
NO PURCHASE NECESSARY

HERE'S HOW THE SWEEPSTAKES WORKS:
The Harlequin Reader Service shipments for January, February and March 1994 will contain, respectively, coupons for entry into three prize drawings: a trip for two to San Francisco, an Alaskan cruise for two and a trip for two to Hawaii. To be eligible for any drawing using an Entry Coupon, simply complete and mail according to directions.

There is no obligation to continue as a Reader Service subscriber to enter and be eligible for any prize drawing. You may also enter any drawing by hand printing your name and address on a 3" x 5" card and the destination of the prize you wish that entry to be considered for (i.e., San Francisco trip, Alaskan cruise or Hawaiian trip). Send your 3" x 5" entries to: Indulge a Little 6947 Sweepstakes, c/o Prize Destination you wish that entry to be considered for, P.O. Box 1315, Buffalo, NY 14269-1315, U.S.A. or Indulge a Little 6947 Sweepstakes, P.O. Box 610, Fort Erie, Ontario L2A 5X3, Canada.

To be eligible for the San Francisco trip, entries must be received by 4/30/94; for the Alaskan cruise, 5/31/94; and the Hawaiian trip, 6/30/94. No responsibility is assumed for lost, late or misdirected mail. Sweepstakes open to residents of the U.S. (except Puerto Rico) and Canada, 18 years of age or older. All applicable laws and regulations apply. Sweepstakes void wherever prohibited.

For a copy of the Official Rules, send a self-addressed, stamped envelope (WA residents need not affix return postage) to: Indulge a Little 6947 Rules, P.O. Box 4631, Blair, NE 68009, U.S.A.

INDR93

INDULGE A LITTLE 6947 SWEEPSTAKES
NO PURCHASE NECESSARY

HERE'S HOW THE SWEEPSTAKES WORKS:
The Harlequin Reader Service shipments for January, February and March 1994 will contain, respectively, coupons for entry into three prize drawings: a trip for two to San Francisco, an Alaskan cruise for two and a trip for two to Hawaii. To be eligible for any drawing using an Entry Coupon, simply complete and mail according to directions.

There is no obligation to continue as a Reader Service subscriber to enter and be eligible for any prize drawing. You may also enter any drawing by hand printing your name and address on a 3" x 5" card and the destination of the prize you wish that entry to be considered for (i.e., San Francisco trip, Alaskan cruise or Hawaiian trip). Send your 3" x 5" entries to: Indulge a Little 6947 Sweepstakes, c/o Prize Destination you wish that entry to be considered for, P.O. Box 1315, Buffalo, NY 14269-1315, U.S.A. or Indulge a Little 6947 Sweepstakes, P.O. Box 610, Fort Erie, Ontario L2A 5X3, Canada.

To be eligible for the San Francisco trip, entries must be received by 4/30/94; for the Alaskan cruise, 5/31/94; and the Hawaiian trip, 6/30/94. No responsibility is assumed for lost, late or misdirected mail. Sweepstakes open to residents of the U.S. (except Puerto Rico) and Canada, 18 years of age or older. All applicable laws and regulations apply. Sweepstakes void wherever prohibited.

For a copy of the Official Rules, send a self-addressed, stamped envelope (WA residents need not affix return postage) to: Indulge a Little 6947 Rules, P.O. Box 4631, Blair, NE 68009, U.S.A.

INDR93

INDULGE A LITTLE
SWEEPSTAKES

OFFICIAL ENTRY COUPON

This entry must be received by: JUNE 30, 1994
This month's winner will be notified by: JULY 15, 1994
Trip must be taken between: AUGUST 31, 1994-AUGUST 31, 1995

YES, I want to win the 3-Island Hawaiian vacation for two. I understand that the prize includes round-trip airfare, first-class hotels and pocket money as revealed on the "wallet" scratch-off card.

Name____

Address ________________________ Apt. ________________

City____

State/Prov.____________________ Zip/Postal Code________________

Daytime phone number_______________________________
(Area Code)

Account #______________________________________

Return entries with invoice in envelope provided. Each book in this shipment has two entry coupons—and the more coupons you enter, the better your chances of winning!

 MONTH3

INDULGE A LITTLE
SWEEPSTAKES

OFFICIAL ENTRY COUPON

This entry must be received by: JUNE 30, 1994
This month's winner will be notified by: JULY 15, 1994
Trip must be taken between: AUGUST 31, 1994-AUGUST 31, 1995

YES, I want to win the 3-Island Hawaiian vacation for two. I understand that the prize includes round-trip airfare, first-class hotels and pocket money as revealed on the "wallet" scratch-off card.

Name____

Address ________________________ Apt. ________________

City____

State/Prov.____________________ Zip/Postal Code________________

Daytime phone number_______________________________
(Area Code)

Account #______________________________________

Return entries with invoice in envelope provided. Each book in this shipment has two entry coupons—and the more coupons you enter, the better your chances of winning!

© 1993 HARLEQUIN ENTERPRISES LTD. MONTH3